# Confessions

## of a

# War Child

A novel
by
Chaker Khazaal

"The characters and situations in this book are entirely fictional and bear no relation to any real person or actual happening.

This book is sold subject to the condition that it shall not, by way of trade or otherwise, be lent, resold, hired-out or otherwise circulated without the publisher's prior consent, in any form or cover other than which is published without a similar condition including this condition being imposed on the subsequent purchaser.

No part of this publication may be reproduced or transmitted in any form or by any means, electronically or mechanically, including photocopying, recording or any information storage or retrieval system, without the prior permission from the publisher. The publisher does not have any control over and does not assume any responsibility for author or third-party Web sites for their content."

Copyright © 2013 Chaker Khazaal. All rights reserved.
Cover art © 2013 Ali Shehadé. Used under license.
ISBN 978-1-4823931-6-3, 1-4823931-6-6

To everyone who has loved and lost...

## Table of Contents

| | |
|---|---|
| Chapter One: The Pearl | 1 |
| Chapter Two: The Friend | 23 |
| Chapter Three: The Lover | 41 |
| Chapter Four: The Troubles | 57 |
| Chapter Five: The Mystery | 73 |
| Chapter Six: The Confusion | 92 |
| Chapter Seven: The Mission | 105 |
| Chapter Eight: The Situation | 125 |
| Chapter Nine: The Reunion | 135 |
| Chapter Ten: The Hardships | 155 |
| Chapter Eleven: The Confessions | 173 |
| Index of Charachters | 194 |
| About the Author | 195 |

Dear Readers,

I was inspired to write this book on 01 July 2012, the same night that a dear friend, Ryan Maiden, left our world. As I sat on my balcony and asked his soul, "Where are you now?" He answered:

*I was wandering the streets in this strange place, as a newcomer trying to find something familiar to remind me of my real world. Then a glorious golden tree adorning a huge house caught my eye. As I gazed into the light on that fall afternoon, a cat on its porch, silent and dignified, stretched and started to purr. A man suddenly appeared at the front door. From down the street he looked strangely elegant and slim, but his clothes were somehow out of fashion. Approaching he bent effortlessly to stroke this beautiful feline creature. His face was peaceful, and his eyes seemed to hide a mystery. He looked unusually young, despite his full head of grey hair. While still stroking his beautiful cat, I took the liberty to address him, "Forgive me, sir, may I ask about your secret that keeps you looking so young?" He then lowered his eyes, looked at me with a smile and replied, "Young man, I have had a life full of joyful and painful experiences, and many interesting encounters; but that life was cut short just into my forties. Every day since then, I tell a story to any young person greeting me upon arriving here. I tell my stories without regret or fear, which allows me to be young and happy forever. Well… it seems that destiny sent you to me today. Welcome to my world, the World of the Dead. Open your heart and mind, and I will tell you a story, the last and greatest one of them all.'*

# Chapter One: The Pearl
*Part One*

It was the last bullet that added the most meaning to my life. It was the bullet that killed me on that fall evening, fired by someone whose identity would take years to discover. I was killed at my wedding ceremony as family and friends gathered around. I always believed in symbols, but never realized that I might end up being part of one.

The wealth I'd accumulated, the fame I'd enjoyed, and all my life experiences were ended by that bullet. It started a war between two towns—my hometown, Saghar, a town built by the wells of the hot Arabian Desert, and our neighbouring town, Kabar. It also killed the dreams I had been making with the woman I loved most in my life, Camilia. She was eloquent, elegant, graceful and had—up to my death—withstood whatever life brought. Unfortunately, this time it was different: she had lost me, too. She lost me in a country not her own, after leaving her family to be with me.

I was born in Saghar in 1905, when the town was still being established by nomads who travelled the desert. They were worried about their future in the midst of an era when European colonial powers were invading our country. My grandfather led one of the tribes that travelled for months looking for a place to settle, far from the violence of colonization. I grew up helping my family with agriculture and dairy production until I turned twenty-two and made my way to France. I had gotten to know a traveller, Eric, who frequently visited Saghar for his research, and I was accepted to the same university where he studied. He helped me apply, and was the first person to ever believe in me. I was granted one of the best scholarships in the country to study engineering. France became my home, and Saghar was where my businesses and family were. At that time in my life, people described me as "bright," while later they would use words like "powerful" and "intimidating."

Camilia was 19 when I met her in 1944, a beautiful tall French girl who radiated positive energy and enthusiasm despite the impact of World War II on her country. I was 20 years older than her, but for us age was never an issue. She was training to become a translator for a private French corporation that provided grants to my production plants. She visited Saghar twice in the same year, capturing my attention and love.

Two years after meeting her, I asked her to marry

me under the Eiffel Tower in Paris. She had one request: she wanted our wedding to be held at a castle in Sahgar's neighbouring town of Kabar. My family and friends agreed to come and celebrate with us. Little did any of us know our wedding ceremony would turn into my funeral.

The bullet was fired at 8:05 p.m. of that 1946 Fall evening, shortly after Camilia became my wife. My chest took it, and my blood turned her dress and the pearls around her neck from white to red. Looking at me in tears, she promised to carry on with my dreams—our dreams—a few seconds after, I passed away. The bullet might have ended everything for me, but it started a new chapter for her and those she would meet along the way from then to now.

So in love, I decided to follow the path she was about to take. Since my death, I've been free to travel into the minds of all people except one: Camilia. Instead I was trapped in her heart, both alive and yet very dead. For the next six decades, Camilia led her journey, struggling to rightfully get what I'd left her in my will and at the same time trying to find out who killed me.

Camilia, my love, I have looked at you every night as you slept, and now feel confident in narrating your story, and telling the world how you redefined possibilities.

*Part Two*

At the age of 87, Camilia lived far from France and Saghar. She had moved ten years ago to an island in the Atlantic Ocean where she was not known to anyone. The mansion she lived in defined her journey.

The living room was inspired by the Arabian Desert, with the sitting area on the floor as she had always preferred, insisting to her sisters that it was better for their backs. They, as Westerners, laughed at her obsession with Arabic culture. And when she married me, they never considered her part of the family again. She was disowned and became a stranger.

Her kitchen was modern because she still enjoyed cooking French meals, which she believed to be the best among world cuisines. She is right, too. I always loved her food—one of the things I miss the most about the world you Readers are in.

The hallway that took you across to the library was covered with photos of her travels around the world. She could be seen with prominent figures—artists, lawyers and people from all walks of life. The legal books in her library further explained her interests: her main missions were to get the rights to the ownership of all my production plants and to learn the identity of my murderer. This is how everyone saw Camilia, a strong woman on a mission.

This evening, Camilia was attending an event, and so she went in every room trying to find the pearl necklace she always kept around her neck. The twelve pearls of the necklace were also the code that opened a safe where Camilia kept a secret. The safe only opened when the twelve pearls were inserted—the *exact* pearls, which cannot be replicated or replaced.

She walked up the stairs elegantly as she always did, and passed by all the rooms that were each inspired by a country she had visited. She was not worried, as she knew the pearl necklace must be somewhere around the house. She remembered looking at it the previous night, and she had again recalled the first time she saw the necklace: I'd bought it for her right before our wedding.

So Camilia raced down the stairs with all the incredible energy she still had, and decided to give up, something she did not do very often. She said aloud to herself: I will wear the diamond one instead; it will shine and Wahab will love it.

I did not like the Wahab comment very much, but neither did I like her giving up and referring to an alternative. This meant she had forgotten something

I'd always reminded her of that: alternatives make your destination even further.

But just as she grabbed her little embroidered purse, she saw the pearl necklace shining by her big wooden Turkish chair. She took off the diamond necklace and put the pearls in her hand. A smile lit up her not-so-wrinkled face and bright grey eyes. She left her house and walked to the corner while attempting to put the pearls on, but her shaky hands failed her, and the pearls fell and scattered upon the old empty street of the island. Camilia panicked, but soon found comfort in a helpful slim young man wandering the streets with a cigarette in his mouth.

Nader was a twenty-four-year-old student at the main university on the island. His study permit was about to expire, and he did not meet the qualifications to become a resident. His scholarship only covered his expenses for one year, and he had no money to support himself after. He was left with the one option he most feared: he was due to return to his hometown, Kabar. It was a place at war full of painful memories. That day, he walked the streets, thinking about his possibilities, looking for something to keep him busy before his class the next day.

Soon Nader approached Camilia with the pearls he'd quickly collected. She thanked him while looking at his big smile and bright eyes. She counted the twelve pearls, repeating that they were very important, that none should go missing.

"You saved my day, young man. If I did not have to meet with a dear friend and attend an event at eight o'clock, I would have invited you for a tea."

Nader grinned and lit his second cigarette as he walked away from Camilia, who then greeted her driver and drove off to meet Wahab. Nader was walking when a sparkle from beneath the lip of the sidewalk winked at him: a pearl from Camilia's necklace had been left behind. He wondered, "But I thought she counted them. I must find her and give her the missing pearl. She said they're important. She probably has to be wearing them for her eight o'clock event. I'll find her. Five hours is plenty of time and I have nothing to do."

Camilia's house was a few steps behind Nader, hidden by a big tree that she loved—largely because it kept her home away from wandering eyes. Had I been able to talk to Nader, I would have told him to look behind, to enter via the gate and leave the pearl by the door. But only much later, I realized that the young man was clumsy and never paid attention to detail. I was suddenly reminded of the philosophy that everything happens for a reason.

He grabbed the pearl with his big hand and walked down the old street of the island, starting a journey to find Camilia. I followed doggedly, for until that afternoon, I had not known the secret locked in the safe. When Camilia dropped the pearl as she got in the car, I was close to losing hope—but I never did.

Camilia had always taught me how to be hopeful in life, and I was constantly reminded of that, even in death.

So many years ago, I had given the pearls to Camilia on a Fall evening while we were walking by the wells of Saghar, right before our wedding. She touched each pearl and smiled at me. Her smile always lit my world, and on that afternoon it radiated in every wall of my heart. She later wore the necklace on our wedding, and took it off for the first time a few days after my murder. She had just returned to France with nothing to live on. She had left her job a few months before, and my family had even taken my savings away from her. She had no money, no family, and no husband.

My oldest brother, Ayham, helped Camilia get out of Saghar. The aftermath of my murder left a grieving wife, an angry family and two towns that would be at war for decades. My family never approved of my desire to marry a foreigner, but they had to accept that it was the choice my heart and mind had already made. They believed that extremists from Kabar had killed me for marrying a woman from a different religion. They blamed Kabar, and blame became war—isn't that how every war always started?

After I died, Camilia arrived in Paris, and her relatives refused to open their homes to her. She took refuge at her friend Paul's tiny apartment and borrowed some francs from him to help get her life back on track. She first needed to buy a safe. It was very important for her to lock away a secret that might help her come to terms with a new reality. I only lived in Camilia's heart, and love is the seed of respect. I did not wish to intrude and to know what she wanted to keep to herself; I loved my Camilia in all the meaning of the word and feeling.

It was a wet day in France, and Camilia walked the streets with tears in her eyes. She went to a shop that sold safes and bought one customized to only open with the twelve pearls I'd given her. This ended up being the same safe that Camilia kept for sixty-six years, and never opened—not even once. I saw her put inside a picture of me, her journal, and a piece of paper she'd scribbled on. It was the secret she wanted to lock away, that even I did not know at that point.

The afternoon she bought the safe, I decided to leave my Camilia and travel the world. I had just been killed and sent away from the love of my life. I was angry, but time healed that wound and I eventually found joy in being a distant observer of life. A few days after my murder, I travelled for a year, escaping from my pain, because seeing Camilia affected me more than that bullet had. But I returned after because I missed her, as I always did when we were apart.

During the following years, Camilia's pearls were a source of both joy and pain. She kept herself together, and was very strong despite everything that life had in store for her. In the depths of her grey eyes there had always been a volcano of emotions ready to erupt, but it never did. She was calm and controlled, above all.

In 1987, Camilia was about to dispose of the pearls and the safe she had bought forty one years ago, a few days after my murder. She was struggling to come to a decision, and I felt totally helpless to the woman I loved so much. She boarded a boat sailing from France to Italy, the home of some of her favourite music and art. She took the safe and the pearls and by all accounts, it appeared she was about to toss them into the sea.

"Damn you, life," she fumed. "What have you given me other than pain? It has been over forty years since you took away the love of my life, and now I constantly struggle with monsters."

Camilia was frustrated largely because of the case she was involved in. Every day for the last forty years, she had been fighting for the right to know who killed me. As my wife, she also had a right to the generous bequeathment I left her in my will. Unfortunately, in a country fighting a war and battling corruption, subsequent papers were forged and Camilia lost her lawful inheritance. She was forced to live off the jobs she was offered translating, but her main commitment remained her legal pursuit.

Thus while having a moment of sadness by the edge of the boat with the safe in her hand, a man approached, asking if she needed any help. Camilia said no, that she was fine. Then she looked at him again, and saw some similarities between my looks and his. Wahab had just decided to run away from the Saghar-Kabar war and move to France. His refugee claim to France was rejected, so he was leaving to try and apply for asylum in Italy.

"Are you sure you're fine? A beautiful and elegant lady like you should be dancing with her husband down in the lounge. Haven't you heard the music?"

Camilia was never one for dancing, and was not shy about expressing that to Wahab. "I don't dance, and perhaps a handsome young man like you should be busy with the ladies downstairs."

Wahab replied with a smile that reminded her of mine. "I'm having a wonderful evening alone before illegally entering Italy. I am taking chances here—starting with this, as you could be an immigration officer and arrest me."

Although I did not enjoy seeing Wahab flirting with my Camilia, I respected the man for talking about chances with her. I always believed that chances are the wheels that move our destiny. And Camilia always appreciated humour, so she walked closer toward Wahab. "You remind me of my husband. He died a long time ago and I was having a moment with him here."

(She was *not* having a moment with me; I don't know why Camilia said that. She was having a moment with herself. Later I learned that Camilia thought of me as part of her, the two of us living together forever. She loved me as much as I loved her, and she missed me as much as well.)

Wahab then looked at the safe. "What is that in your hand?"

"It's my pearl necklace and a little box that I carry around. I was about to throw it deep into the sea, but then fate sent you, young man. You remind me of him so much that I think of our encounter as a message from life."

I wanted to tell Camilia that it was also a message from *me*, although I would have preferred it to be delivered by someone less attractive and appealing than Wahab. I was scared he would take my Camilia and make her part of his life. I wanted Camilia to be happy, but jealousy followed me even in death. I believe that jealousy is a symptom of misbalance in our lives. I always wished I had more time with my Camilia, and thus that was where my misbalance came from.

"Well," Wahab began, "you mentioned that you don't dance, but would you honor me with a glass of wine downstairs? It's a lovely evening. Let me put this necklace around your neck too; I am sure it looks better on you than it would deep down in the sea."

Camilia accepted Wahab's invitation to have a drink, but gently declined his offer to put the necklace around her neck. Instead she put it on with her own firm but soft hands, and walked down to the second level of the boat with him.

The two had a lovely evening, especially after Camilia found out that Wahab and I were from the same town. She did not tell him who I was, the man whose murder caused the Saghar-Kabar war. He flirted with her constantly; however, she did not let it go further than a friendly encounter. I was proud of my Camilia, for she still treasured our love like I did.

Wahab began to talk about the war between Saghar and Kabar. Camilia avoided the topic, as she always preferred not to speak about it. I assumed the war reminded her of me, something she kept to herself.

Camilia had two suitcases and the small safe when she departed the boat. Wahab helped carry her luggage and they walked towards the immigration officers at the port. Wahab said, "May I touch the pearls and this box you are carrying, Camilia? They are the reason we met, and I feel I have now made a lifelong friend."

"You may absolutely touch them. Good luck, young man."

"We talked for a whole evening, but I never got to tell you that I am not as young as I look," he said.

Camilia smiled. "When I speak of your age, I never think about the time you have served in life, only about your spirit."

The two walked toward the port, and Wahab made his way into Italy. His claim was approved, and a few years later, he received his Italian citizenship. He became a successful businessman, known for his charisma and good looks. He remained a good friend to Camilia and over the years would visit her in some of the many places she lived, even as far away as the island in the Atlantic. She told him little about herself, and almost nothing about *me*. She preferred to listen to Wahab's stories and be there to advise him when he required it. She was his friend of mystery, and he enjoyed the little he explored.

After that evening, Camilia decided she would never get rid of the safe or the pearls, but would protect them with her life. Thus, she sent a challenge to the universe. Sipping tea in Italy later that day, Camilia decided that if she and the pearls made it through life together, her secret should come out after she died. If they did not, this was the path the universe had set for her and a secret would be brought to the World of the Dead with her.

My lovely Camilia always lived by symbols and mystery. She had always been a mastermind for success and I never doubted she would be the best choice running the company I'd left behind. Her mind and mine were connected, just like each pearl of that necklace was joined together for a purpose.

But now the twelfth pearl was in the hands of Nader, the young man originally from Kabar, who had arrived on the island a few months before running into Camilia. Nader was a smart young fellow who had been granted a scholarship for a one-year program. He'd gladly fled the war between Saghar and Kabar, also leaving a secret buried in his hometown. As his immigration status did not allow him to work, he spent his days after classes walking around the streets, meeting people, listening to their stories but keeping his to himself. He was in a foreign place and felt uncomfortable trusting anyone. The people of the island were very friendly, welcoming all guests and visitors. They were busy with their jobs, but enjoyed having evenings and weekends off. The island was known for hosting events bringing people from all around the world.

Nader was thus spurred on to find Camilia, and began his journey at an internet café a few steps away from her house. He did not want to turn the pearl in to the local police station, although the thought had crossed his mind—he wanted to deliver it personally. He feared that the police wouldn't take the matter seriously. He thought of the beginning of his plan: find all the events happening on the island at eight o'clock that night. But this idea was brought to a standstill by the first setback: there were over one hundred events taking place on the island at eight o'clock that night.

But whenever he was challenged with a setback in life, Nader thought about people who had faced storms to arrive at their destination. He thought about Abraham Lincoln, who failed many challenges before becoming the president of the United States of America. Nader had carried a piece of newspaper in his wallet with an article that reminded him of moving forward in life and never giving up. "Hard storms make great sailors", he mumbled to himself.

Nader did not know where the insistence on finding

Camilia came from. It was a feeling he had, and he decided to follow his heart. "If I don't find her by eight o'clock, I will convince the police to contact me when they find her, and hopefully I will still be on the island. Or I can go back to where I met her: she has to return there eventually."

Once again, I was seeing someone starting to contemplate alternatives. He was speaking his mind aloud when Riad, a handsome young man, saw the wandering young fellow muttering to himself.

Riad said, "So if I understand correctly, you found what you think is an expensive jewel, you want to be a good citizen and return it to the owner, and you thought this might be done by *Googling* it?

Nader looked back at Riad and didn't know what to reply. He was intimidated by the tall lad, who, unlike the rest of the island's citizens, seemed rude and unfriendly.

(I would have told Nader to never judge a book by its cover, but I figured he would have learned that through his travels.)

Nader finally decided to answer in his usual friendly way and explained the story of the pearl to Riad.

Riad had recently moved to the island, leaving his family behind in Kabar. I know what you're thinking, Readers, yet it is *not* a small world, but a huge world where everything happens for a reason. Riad listened to an inner voice that asked him to initiate a conversation with Nader.

Riad, a film student, was an activist for refugees' rights and an advocate to stop the war between Saghar and Kabar. He saw a light in Nader's eyes that he wanted to further investigate. He knew that people hid behind their smiles, and via some conversational trickery, he did not hesitate to discover more about Nader. "Would you like me to help you? I have a couple of hours to kill before I must go to an all-night protest at Parliament Hill."

Nader was an activist himself, having been a refugee since birth. Although born in Kabar, his grandparents had fled the war back in their home country, the Republic of Idel. Riad's response made Nader question his usual doubt that asking for help was a waste of time. I think it was the first time Nader learned that when you need something in life, you need to ask for it. It all starts by asking ourselves what we want, then life brings people to assist us with the journey.

Nader accepted Riad's help and they left the internet café in search of Camilia. Nader squeezed the pearl in his hand as he looked up at the tall man standing beside him, now his partner on the journey to find my Camilia.

Oh, Camilia, if you only knew how many people were constantly in search of you! I was one of the lucky ones to have found you in life, but one of the unlucky ones to have lost you on that Fall evening. There was so much more I wanted to do with you, and never had the chance…

Meanwhile, Camilia had noticed the missing pearl when she left the car. She was on her way to the restaurant to meet Wahab, who was visiting the island once again. Camilia's fear and panic were soon softened by Wahab's voice. "This should be marked as an important day in history—you're actually late."

"It is not the time for your humour, young man; I just lost one of the pearls."

Wahab shrugged. "So you have eleven now. He will surely forgive you for losing one after sixty-six years."

"No, young man, there must be twelve or they are just a piece of jewellery that holds a memory."

"But isn't that what they are?"

This was one of the first times Wahab had heard Camilia raise her voice with aggravation. Even when he'd met her on the boat almost twenty-five years ago, she was not in such a panic. Now he gave her a hug, and listened to her talk of what happened earlier when the necklace broke.

Finally he said, "It is simple then. We will finally have our late lunch, go for a walk before the event, and then report the incident at the police station. They will catch the thief who kept the pearl and you will have it back."

Wahab was mocking Camilia, who did not catch up on that and thought he was serious about going to the police.

Camilia insisted, "No, the young fellow is not a thief. The pearl could have fallen near my house and

I will find it tomorrow morning—if it is meant to be found."

Camilia recalled Nader's face, which brought her comfort and joy. Her inner voice started telling her that if the pearl was lost, then so was what she kept in the safe, and that it would be the right time to throw the safe deep in the sea where it might very well belong. After all, I was gone, and all that belonged to me did not matter—except her love to me, which was always kept in her heart.

The same pearl that Camilia kept safe over the years now had a meaning associated with a stranger she met on the street. As long as it brought her peace that afternoon, I was happy. Since I met Camilia, I always wanted her to be happy. And for once, I could see that in her eyes, hear it in her sighs, and feel it with every heartbeat as she walked with Wahab to the restaurant.

"I am ready to eat, young man, and I have a feeling that it is a going to be a good meal. It is a French restaurant, after all."

"You never change, my friend, you never change," chuckled Wahab.

But Wahab was mistaken. I had sensed many changes in my Camilia since I'd left the world. When I first met her, she was very soft and full of life. After my murder, she became stiff and rarely showed any emotions. People were only able to feel passion through her eyes, which never lied. They were always able to feel her pain, which I believed to be caused by my murder.

Camilia and Wahab walked into the French restaurant that she frequented. Surprisingly, she was not thinking about the pearl anymore, I would only know why a few hours later.

Wahab was telling Camilia about the never ending war between Saghar and Kabar. She tried to avoid the subject, changing the topic several times during her time with him.

I knew exactly who killed me, and I always wished it had never started a war between two towns that had previously been living in peace. War had killed the joy of several generations, and it carried stories, like every other war did.

So I will now tell the story of a war child—and that's anyone born into violence, or who later becomes part of it. War is not only global, it is also local and can be found even in what seems to be the most peaceful corner of the world.

# Chapter Two: The Friend

I always heard people say that the world is a small place whenever they encountered what they saw as a coincidence. Being dead now, I don't see a small world of coincidences, but a large world with people shaping their destiny through every encounter. The day Camilia lost her pearl, I saw a living example of this with Nader and Riad's meeting. I had seen Riad around the island whenever I was checking on my Camilia, which was almost every day. He was also from Kabar and had moved to the island to escape both the war and a tragedy that had happened to him. Nader, the Idel refugee from Kabar, did not know this until a conversation between the two started.

Riad asked, "So, where are you from?"

Nader said, "I am from Idel, but was born and grew up in Kabar as a refugee. Do you know where that is?"

"Of course I do. I am from Kabar too. I grew up in the south part, bordering Saghar."

Nader raised his eyebrows. "That's a rough area. I am from the centre."

Riad lit a match. "My brother used to live there."

"Where does he live now?"

Riad did not answer. Instead he lit his cigarette, and before continuing the conversation, he thought about his brother whom he had lost to violence before leaving for the island. He was found killed at a site a few miles away from the centre of Kabar, and ever since then Riad had been looking for answers. The government of Kabar did not help in the investigation because of the war, and a wound was left open, causing constant pain in Riad's life. The government had confirmed that the murder was a result of a fight, which Riad never believed. Little did he know that he was finally close to the answers he sought—as close as Nader was to him. Like with Camilia, the death of a loved one caused a purpose in his life that he had not given up on. Life brings questions so that the universe can create a mission for us to find the answers. Riad's journey to his answers was about to take a new turn when the conversation between the two Kabar natives continued.

Nader confessed, "I grew up in the worst time during the Saghar-Kabar war, and spent my life seeing two countries fighting. War stole my childhood. I don't remember playing with toy cars like I see children do in movies. I only recall running from one bomb shelter to another. This is happening again, and as we speak, generations are losing their lives holding onto the thinnest strand of hope left. It is history repeating itself. My grandparents moved from Idel to Kabar because of war, only to face another one. Idel refugees get it the worst, having no access to public services like schools or hospitals."

Riad agreed. "When a Nation admits its mistakes, it then begins its journey to solutions. People of Kabar and Saghar must come to peace, and Idel refugees should be given equal rights whether in Kabar, Saghar or elsewhere. Everyone, including the international community, has made mistakes. But in a world of love and forgiveness, mistakes can be called experiences."

Nader frowned. "You are right, so what are they waiting for?"

"They are making more money! What is war?"

Nader thought. "It is fighting, it is violent."

Riad scoffed. "It is also a moneymaking machine for people who have interests beyond what we see. War is the state where communities go into panic, and the people become vulnerable, only looking to survive."

"Well, if war is a business, then are we the products or the consumers?"

Riad smiled, but it had a touch of a grimace. "Some of us become consumers, and others become products."

"What is the difference?"

"A consumer finds fulfillment as a product is being used. They are both at the merchant's mercy. Some people from Kabar and Saghar have used the war to their own benefits, and these are the consumers. These are the ones that make things worse. They want war, and when we want something, we create it. The products are the people, like you, me, and our families and friends."

Nader nodded his approval, but his sigh was a sign of hidden stories. Nader sounded like a simple young man, but no book in life should be judged by its cover. Up to that point, Riad did not know that when opening the book that was in front of him, the answers he looked for since the death of his brother would be found, wrapped in simplicity, hiding a complex past that war had created. War is a poison that destroys places and lives, and corruption becomes one of its grown seeds.

Before meeting Camilia I lived my life hiding behind my smile, holding onto the sadness of being lonely, despite the great things I had. I, unlike Riad, knew what Nader was hiding, and his last sentence before getting back to the pearl would be something that Riad would never get a chance to understand.

Nader said, "War also creates monsters. Monsters steal lives, take childhoods and destroy homes."

Kabar is a town that is as old as Saghar, for both were built around the same time by related nomads. Kabar is known for its oil, and so it is a town that many governments and corporations have a vested interest in. Saghar is famous for its many production plants.

From the time of their founding to the time of my murder, Kabar and Saghar had always been at peace.

On my birthday when I turned 18, a few friends convinced me to go against my father's will and travel with them by foot to Kabar. I lied to my father, saying that we were going to camp in the desert, closer to Saghar. My father was always protective and feared for us due to the colonizer's army that travelled the desert at night sometimes.

We walked to Kabar without having to cross borders like there are today. We arrived at dawn, when men were going to the oil plants and women were heading to the markets where products from Saghar were sold.

Kabar was also known for its castle, built by the nomads who first arrived in the area and nestled close to the oil plants where everyone in the town worked. The castle was our destination and people guided us there. It was the same castle where my wedding was held years later. I can never forget the conversation I had with Abu Khalil, a Kabar native who sat outside of his shop that sold books. He was an old man and probably one of the first people to arrive in Kabar. We asked him for directions on our way:

"Excuse me, is this the way to the castle?"

"Where are you from?" Abu Khalil asked us.

"We are from Saghar and looking for the castle, are we in the right direction?"

"You are. You will have to walk on this path until

you get there. You will pass by few markets, make a right after and you will arrive at the castle."

We thanked him and prepared to start walking again when he stopped us. "I have a favour to ask you. You should know that this castle is a symbol of the birth of Kabar, and Saghar too. It resists everything and stands to remind us of our fathers' dream to stay away from colonization and live freely here, in peace.."

I said, "We can't wait to see it. What is your favour?"

"Just to remember it as you grow up, and protect it. Colonization and war are diseases, and diseases spread."

"Don't you worry," I reassured him, "we will not allow war to come close to here, or the castle."

"War doesn't come and go; it grows from anger and acts on a stage of violence. I feel that anger is coming our way. Never let anger numb your minds, it will grow and destroy generations."

I did not understand a word, and my friends were starting to get bored of the old man lecturing us with his mysterious warnings. I apologized, thanked Abu Khalil for his assistance, and joined my friends who had already walked away from us. We arrived at the castle and met with young men from Kabar who gave us food and a place to stay for the night. They celebrated my birthday, and we stayed up late that night making our way back to Saghar in the early hours of the morning.

Little did I know that Abu Khalil was feeling the danger that arrived twenty-three years after I had first met him. It occurred a second after I left the world. On that day, a few hours after dying, I ran into Abu Khalil here. It was only the second time I'd seen him after many years, yet I had no difficulties recognizing him. He was one of the first people I saw in the World of the Dead. He welcomed me, saying: "I met you over twenty years ago, do you remember me?"

Still adjusting to my surroundings, I said, "I do, the man on the way to the castle."

"They killed you, then?"

"They did, on my wedding day."

"I saw that. Do you know who killed you?"

I nodded. "The man who killed me is from Kabar, your hometown."

"Then our people are going to fight. I felt that years ago. I saw it in your eyes. The castle will witness bloody fights. Promise me that we will remain friends, even when our people are in conflict."

I frowned. "But your people just took the joy of my life—they sent me here way too early and left a broken-hearted widow."

Abu Khalil, who later became a close friend (and one day I hope he narrates his story to you as well), took me over Saghar and Kabar, then told me about the motives of my murder, and explained what would take more lives from both towns and later from both countries. He had a vision when he looked into my eyes years ago. He did not know that he was looking at the core of the war's cause, but he felt it. Intuition is the third eye that we each have and only get to use at a moment when the present is merging with the realm where time does not exist. It comes as a gift and leaves a glimpse into a world that doesn't know coincidences.

Abu Khalil and I met on several occasions and became close friends, always observing the life we left together from a distance. One of the differences between your world and the World of the Dead is that things learned here are based on observations; while for you, it should always be sought beyond that. I wish that the people from the world I had come from could do the same: build friendships even if their governments fought. Friendship creates dialogue, and communication is a key to solutions. In the world you, the Readers, live in, things are not as simple as they are to us here. Some governments and private corporations have found benefits in the misery of the nations, and purposefully made things complex. When things are not understood, they are feared. It is how I view the politics of the world I left. I feel it is like a chess game, played with people instead of pawns. For many years I hoped that the cruel game between Saghar and Kabar would end, for the sake of all people, but until today my wish has not come true.

War is not only defined by the fighting between two parties, it extends to the souls of people. It destroys dreams, ruins generations, and displaces people from their homes. Nader and Riad were two examples of people who fled the violence, seeking their right to live in peace.

Nader suddenly remembered that it had been thirty minutes since he first met Riad, and time to find Camilia was running out. "I am starting to get worried about the pearl."

Riad then looked at the papers Nader had printed out from the internet café. Although he was reading the pages in front of him, his mind was now in Kabar and Saghar, just like mine. He was also thinking about his brother. Riad returned back from his thoughts and looked at Nader and the papers in his hands. "What are these?"

Nader said, "This is a list of all events happening on the island at eight tonight. It is already late; I can't go to all these places looking for her, I won't have enough time."

Riad took his time reading through the papers and then finally said, "Do you have a pen? I want to cross out every event I am sure that an eighty-something-year-old woman will not attend." Riad then started crossing out events like raves, pop concerts, and places where an "elegant and well-spoken" lady, as Nader had described her, would not likely be. "Here you go; I narrowed it down for you to almost thirty events. We should get a map from the store up the street and a coffee while we are at it. I'll point out to you where the thirty events are. They all happen in the same few areas."

Nader felt hopeful. "Thank you, will that take a lot of time?"

"Ask if it will take us to a lot of results, and I will tell you maybe. Time is relative, my friend."

It was a lesson Nader was reminded of by his new friend: When we stress about time, we forget about the results that have to be achieved. Time becomes the main tool of fear. We forget about the journey. This is how stress shatters dreams.

Riad explained further, "Fear is false evidence appearing real. Don't be scared of time, be engaged in your plan to get where you are heading and enjoy the journey as long as it lasts. And now we are heading to get a map and a coffee."

So the two walked, talking again about Idel refugees and the war between Saghar and Kabar. Nader and Riad agreed that governments should be fair in treating the displaced people who lost their homes in Idel decades ago. As for the war, they were at a loss for words and thoughts. They viewed it as a complicated situation, when it was actually much easier than they both imagined. War is created because of a reason, whether bad or good, but conflict blinds people and violence becomes an obstacle to reach peace.

Nader mused, "Peace begins with a healthy and clean dialogue and a new page, just a new page."

As he said this they reached a store that sold the island's maps, and as they made their way in, the two were caught by what the radio was announcing: *"A rainstorm is expected to hit the island tonight, and many events have been cancelled. For a list of cancelled events and functions, please visit the island's website."*

Riad said, "Damn your luck, if her event is one of the cancelled. I know ours won't be: our protest is happening, rain or shine."

Nader was made nervous by the rain and his thwarted plans. He said, "A thought can create a reality, so may I ask that you change your thought to something else? I want to remain positive because I have a feeling that I will run into this lady again to give her the pearl myself."

Riad sighed. "I will not go through this list again to narrow it down for you to cancelled and non-cancelled events. Get your map—it's only two dollars—and find your way. You could also just leave this, and come with me to my protest and forget about this lady and the pearl."

Nader thanked Riad for his time, disappointed because the two were parting ways.

Riad said, "I will follow your words, young man, and think positive. Good luck finding her and let me know if you ever need help here." Riad did not know it but he was not only leaving Nader, he was abandoning his only chance left, up to then, to find answers about the murder of his brother.

There were many mysteries that were unsolved while I lived, and they made a big part of my purpose in life. I only found out the answers when I came to the World of the Dead.

Nearby, Camilia was having a glass of wine before her meal when she heard about the rainstorm. Wahab called and made sure that the event they were attending was still happening. He reported, "The plan is still as it is, eat, then a walk under an umbrella, and the event after."

"I am thinking about the pearl again."

"Why is it so very important? Buy another one and complete the necklace. He will not know the difference anyway, being dead."

"Your humour is not appreciated in this matter. I either find the pearl or give up the necklace."

Wahab rolled his eyes. "As you please. How have you been otherwise?"

Camilia shrugged. "I enjoy my morning walks, the books I read, and the music I listen to."

"But when will you give up the loneliness you are living in?"

Camilia smiled. "Who told you I am lonely?"

"You barely see anyone. You should be enjoying all the wealth that took you tens of years to recover."

"What wealth?" Camilia said seriously.

Wahab thought that Camilia had started to lose her memory when she answered him thus. She did not want to talk about selling all the production plants I owned after winning the case ten years ago, right before moving to the island. It was a subject that brought pain to her. Fifty-six years after my death, Camilia had finally been granted ownership of all the assets I left, but it was such a long, hard road.

I was the happiest person in the World of the Dead when my oldest brother Ayham finally testified that Camilia and I had gotten married before I died, and revealed the real will that I'd left. That original document was kept hidden by my mother, and then passed to my brother. She did not want anything from me to be destroyed, not even the evidence of what they did. Too bad I was dead; I would have loved to celebrate with Camilia over a French dinner and a bottle of wine.

My brother Ayham simply woke up one morning to find himself sunk in guilt. He started talking to me. Funny that, as I never would have been interested in talking to him. He was the one who bullied me when I was a child for having big ears. If I were able to talk to someone, I would have talked to Ghassan, my other brother who was the closest to me.

But again, we choose to give meaning to what we see, and Ayham gave that voice a meaning related to me, his brother. The voice told him to speak the truth and help Camilia. At a very old age, and in bad health, battling a disease, Ayham got in touch with her that same day. A few months after, the production plants were at last granted to Camilia. I was shocked when she decided to sell them to a third party, but I never judged her, and was always confident that she knew better than I did. She probably feared the war, but again, I don't know how to judge my Camilia. I only know how to love her. This is how I have been, living and dead. I always looked for the best in her, and chose never to look at anything in a negative way. Love seeks light, not darkness.

After a case that many politicians and lawyers were part of, Camilia won in court proving that she was my wife by presenting the real documents my brother had given her. A month after I was killed, and in the midst of the war starting between Saghar and Kabar, my mother talked to the family lawyer who had helped me write my will. They agreed that he would receive a large sum of money if the documents were forged and an edited will presented to the courts.

The entire family conspired to deprive Camilia from her rights enshrined in the will. Her determination was the only thing they had to face. Every night I stared at those big grey eyes, I predicted that my family was facing the impossible. Camilia *never* gave up, and she never allowed anyone to take her rights away. The government of Saghar assisted my family, becoming their partners in the crime of changing my will.

My production plants were like the castle of Kabar, they stood facing all the fights that were happening. Four out of the five buildings were turned into shelters, and one was still producing the dairy products that were exported everywhere but to Kabar. Foreign corporations bought the products on the cheap, using the war as an excuse. People in Saghar were desperate and sold products at any price offered. However, the production plant still made a fortune, though not as much as it would have made if there were no war, or if I were still alive.

The waiter interrupted by bringing the plates with Camilia's favourite French meal, beef bourguignon. She cut the meat slowly and said, "I miss him. This is his wealth, not mine. My wealth is sitting down with you, walking around the island and attending cultural and artistic events. My wealth is by doing what he wanted to do, so when we talk about his money, it is not about me."

My Camilia was saying nothing but the truth. If I were still alive, I would be living on an island like she did. I had told her that it was my wish after retirement. We had made plans together for many years in the future, not knowing that a bullet would soon end them all.

Wahab started eating, then paused to speak. "He left it for you. You fought for it. It is yours."

Camilia looked at Wahab, but could only think of the missing pearl and Nader's face. That young man's eyes left warmth in her heart and a smile on her face. I could feel from her heartbeat that she was thinking about the war between Saghar and Kabar, not knowing yet that Nader had been a child of that war since birth. She was reminded of it constantly, whenever she saw news about the fighting. It had started in 1946 on that Fall evening, and it did not end until today. It took so many lives, all because of senseless blame.

Nader, on the other hand, did not know where to begin. Once again, he was confused in the middle of the unknown, something he'd grown up with. Having been a refugee since birth, life had always been unknown to him. He was born in Kabar, a country not his. He knew as growing up that after graduation, he will not be able to work. Laws in Kabar did not permit refugees to have a job as the limited employment opportunities were only for the natives. On the other hand, Kabar officials believed that refugees should not settle so that they don't give up their right to return to their home countries. I never understood what I call the refugee equation where the right of return becomes a mask that hides other rights. It had left millions of refugees in hard conditions with unfair treatment, and uncertainty about their lives. Nader had a plan with a close friend to leave Kabar after he'd graduated high school. Life, with many unknowns along the way, was different than what he had planned. Now as Nader was dubious about his next move, nothing mattered but the pearl.

The pearl was like Nader: it belonged *somewhere*, but had been placed elsewhere. Its existence was based on hope and the creation of a journey to reach its target: the rest of the pearls.

The island had quite a few immigrants; they had

come over the years from all over the world. Many Idel refugees and people from Saghar and Kabar found a safe refuge on the island. They never fought there, unlike back in their homes. As Nader walked the streets trying to reach his goal, another immigrant walked by. Leo was an Italian whose family moved to the island a couple of years ago. The twenty-five-year-old was studying medicine as per his parents' wishes. He was depressed because of all the pressure imposed by his religious and very conservative family.

Leo was bored that afternoon and had left his home to be alone, away from his family. I have always appreciated boredom as much as I enjoyed the adventure that followed. When we live in a state of apathy, the desire for adventure intensifies to become the force that pushes us into a new page of being. Leo's trigger into a conversation with Nader was the outcome of a strong desire that existed in him and unconsciously pushed him into a new path.

Leo's life was full of disappointments. He'd wanted to become a politician, but he was forced to study medicine. He'd wanted to live on another island and have new experiences away from his family, but he was forced to stay in their home until he married, which was not anytime soon, if you asked him.

Creating limits is giving one's dreams a lifetime prison sentence, and here was another young man with shattered dreams, bound by fears and what he saw as failures. He was strolling around enjoying the solitude he frequently chose to be in, when he saw Nader for the first time.

And soon, Leo's life would also change by being part of a night that would redefine many destinies.

## Chapter Three: The Lover

Nader stood in the street holding onto the pearl and looking at the papers Riad had edited by crossing out all the events that an old lady wouldn't attend. Nader muttered, "Half an hour with him and this is how it ends. He left thirty events to choose from, great!"

Leo heard him and said, "What events are you choosing from? I heard you getting all bent out of shape."

Nader was embarrassed. "Long story, I don't know where to begin."

"Start from the end, then explain yourself. And if you find me sleeping out of boredom, wake me up."

Nader appreciated humour, and was encouraged to start a conversation with Leo, introducing himself and telling him about the pearl and the woman he was looking for.

Leo said, "I don't think you can do this in less than four hours. You need years to find a stranger at an event on this island."

Nader reacted to Leo's pessimistic response with spontaneous passion: "I am not giving up!"

His answer intrigued Leo who was looking for something to do that afternoon. "Well then, may I look for her with you?"

Nader was questioning whether he should accept a new person's help. He said, "I would only be losing another half hour. I would be left with 3 hours and 45 minutes to find her."

Leo laughed. "Talk about being negative. Hypocrite."

"Are you calling me a hypocrite?" Nader challenged.

"I don't see another person here in front of me. You were talking about sticking to your goal of finding this pearl woman, yet you think of my encounter as a loss of time." Leo started to walk away when Nader finally decided to ask for help, one of the lessons he was learning through this journey: "I never got your name, and yes, I could stand to take on a partner trying to find who you call the pearl lady."

Leo was hoping for this. Like Nader, he was adventurous and looked for new experiences in his life. He was always faced by his family's restrictions, and now found himself free to embark on what he predicted to be a simple journey. (He was horribly mistaken.) "My name is Leonardo Digiorno Piccillia Molinaro Conti, but you can call me Leo."

Nader's eyes grew wide. "Leo it is, how do you expect me to remember all these names?"

Leo smiled. "I love the way you say my name. Your accent makes it sound so captivating."

Nader changed the subject. "So what do I do now? Which event do I go to? I don't have much time left."

"Why do you keep thinking about what you *don't* have if you are Mr. Positive all the time and never giving up", Leo teased.

"Because a lady is missing her pearl and she said it is very important. Time is running out."

Leo said, "I have heard the story, and I say the pearl lady can live with a pearl missing. It's a *pearl*. Don't make your life harder than it is and it will become easier. You are already looking for her, so live the journey while you think about the purpose but don't let it overtake you."

By now the rainstorm was moving towards the island and the wind was getting stronger and colder by the minute. Leo and Nader walked as the former joked around and the latter worried and thought about finding my Camilia.

Meanwhile, Camilia was finishing her meal with Wahab. They were both silent as they ate, and she was occasionally looking at him with those grey eyes. I can never forget the first time I saw Camilia and those same eyes that never aged, only got richer and deeper with untold stories.

It was in 1944, when she had just arrived in Saghar

for an internship with a private French company. She and the delegation whom she was accompanying stayed at the local hotel, Bayt Al Madina. Bayt Al Madina was built by my uncle for the travellers who stopped in Saghar on their desert journeys. Researchers and foreigners also stayed at the four-room hotel that was as old as my brother Ghassan, born five years after me.

When my family settled in Saghar, my uncle set up a tent that travellers could rent in exchange of whatever they were able to offer. This tent would later become Bayt Al Madina, where my Camilia first stayed. The hotel doesn't exist anymore, as this symbol of Saghar's past and my family itself was bombed a few years ago in the war.

Everyone in Saghar heard that a young woman was coming with the delegation. Mothers sat down with their sons to remind them of how to avoid the "foreign girl" who was coming their way. Oum Issam, Saghar's well-known psychic, told my mother that afternoon: "This girl will take your son. He has lived his life where she is, and you will not stop him from falling in love with her."

My mother came to talk to me that evening. I was 39 then, and had lived seventeen years in France, visiting Saghar regularly to check on my businesses. She began, "There is a girl from France coming with this delegation. Be careful, I heard she is young and single. You can't marry a foreigner."

I laughed at my mother, not knowing that Oum Issam and she were right. My mother was afraid because back then it was a taboo to marry someone foreign or from another religion.

So Camilia arrived in Saghar on a horse cart that only transported the nobles of the country. She wore a hat to protect herself from the sun, and a yellow dress that still shines in my eyes. Everyone in Saghar was waiting to meet the first female foreigner ever to visit our little conservative community.

The year 1944 was a blessed one for Saghar in many ways, aside from Camilia's arrival. French companies had provided us with investment grants and loans to build the community, and helped construct the first school in our town. The children of Saghar no longer had to travel to Kabar to attend their classes. Saghar was being discovered by other nomads who travelled the desert, making it a popular stop on their long trips. The economy boomed, and Saghar was one of the most prosperous towns in the area. Many production plants opened in Saghar that year, but my dairy production plant remained the largest.

I lived in France and stayed in Saghar for one month a year. In August of 1944, I met Camilia when I joined the nobles of Saghar to welcome the French delegation that was about to give further grants and support to our plants. Suddenly, there were her grey eyes looking at me with an expression that I had never encountered until then. She quickly looked away when

I caught her staring. She was with a group of three French men who did not allow my Camilia to speak while they talked about their plans for Saghar and its businesses.

Then, I heard that gentle voice for the first time, bringing a melody of love across a room filled with people. "Excuse me gentlemen, I am tired from our travels and don't want to be rude, but I need to sleep. May I leave to my room now?"

The men in the room each nodded in agreement, some saying words in the native language that Camilia probably did not understand. It was my opportunity to start a conversation with this lady whom Oum Issam, the psychic, was for once right about. I translated the words of the other men, and offered to give Camilia a tour of Saghar in the morning, once she was fully rested.

She agreed. "Thank you. I will be ready in the lobby at nine o'clock."

I did not want to say goodbye to her, but I had to, and my fellow Saghar gentlemen did not miss a chance to make fun of me, having noticed that I was now smitten.

It was another twelve hours before I saw her again. I went home to read a book about Saghar so that I had enough stories to share with Camilia. I also decided that Fatima, a neighbour who was as old as Camilia, I assumed, might join us, so that the people of Saghar would not get any wrong ideas. I still respected the culture of Saghar after travelling Europe and making France my home. I felt stupid for not sharing with Camilia the fact that I lived in Paris, but then she did not ask why I spoke French fluently.

I spent that night thinking about the conversations I was going to have with Camilia the next day. I prepared the stories I would tell her about Saghar and my travels. I didn't dare to ask my mother to iron my shirt, because she would have sensed what she most feared: her son falling in love with a foreigner.

Ironing the shirt was not the challenge, but making a good impression on Camilia despite being twice her age was my concern. After all, I truly believed in love at first sight, just like in the books I had read.

The next morning, after a sleepless night, I met Camilia who was well-rested and looked as beautiful, if not more so, as when I first saw her. She said, "The air here is very fresh, I feel great." Until then, I was feeling horrible being restless and nervous, but when I saw those grey eyes, I felt like I have been sleeping all my life and just woke up to the most beautiful face. I was full of energy and excitement, which I did not want to show so that I keep myself a solid gentleman.

I couldn't help but complementing her, in French of course, on how beautiful she looked. Her cheeks turned rosy, and I knew she was the woman I would one day marry.

I became like Oum Issam, and predicted that she would always be beautiful, something I said during the tour I gave her. I made sure not to miss any detail that would impress Camilia. I thought I saw a deep joy in her eyes when she learned I lived in France.

Love at first sight became the title of the new chapter I was about to open. And thus we walked in the desert, followed by Fatima who was at loss as to why I'd brought her along.

Although 68 years have passed since that day, I was reminded of it by looking at Camilia who was thinking about the pearl.

The pearl was creating a journey for Nader walking with his new partner who did not stop mocking and teasing him. Leo found joking as his way to attract some happiness and positivity into his life.

He asked, "If you don't find her by eight, you can always turn it into the police station, you know that, right?"

Nader said, "I thought about that, but I grew up not liking to use the word 'if.'"

Leo giggled. "Look at you, little philosopher! I was joking about the police, you idiot. The police will fine you for wasting their time. But tell me, where did you learn that philosophy lesson from?"

Nader didn't feel like joking. "I am not a philosopher; I am just looking for the pearl lady. Do you want to help me or not?"

"Can we talk about this inside somewhere, like this coffee shop? The wind is strong." So Nader and Leo walked into a café and each ordered a coffee. Leo told

Nader a little about his life. Nader was starting to think about his waste of time when he was reminded by his inner voice that nothing is a waste but an experience being lived. He also remembered to apply the philosophy that a thought creates the reality desired. If he thought positively, he was then closer to finding my Camilia.

Leo was talking about the coming rainstorm and the difficulties awaiting Nader when he was interrupted once again by Nader asking, "Which event among these would your mother go to?"

"None, she is too busy to go to events other than those related to her work."

"And what are those?"

Leo tapped his cup against the table. "My mother is not the focus, your pearl lady is. My mother doesn't wear pearls." Leo had many issues with his mother having to always live up to her expectations. He never got to do what he enjoyed in his life because he was always preoccupied with what his parents wanted him to do. At a young age, he enjoyed soccer and always wished to be part of the school's team, playing every Sunday. He never got the opportunity to do so because he was urged to attend church, something he still did not believe in.

This is what I notice in many parents of the world you Readers live in. They act as though parenting was a job from God, and their children the products to be developed in an environment of expectations. They forget that their kids are a gift to be appreciated the way they are. Leo did not want to move to the island, but his parents had the final word. He instead wanted to travel the world and settle in his hometown in Italy.

Nader was worried about the time that was racing before the eight o'clock event. He explained his desire to Leo: "When you have a dream that you can accomplish, why abandon the chances to do so? You would be defeating the purpose of living."

Leo roared with glee. "Jesus Christ! Where did you learn this one from?"

Nader remained serious. "From the refugee camps I lived in. Never give up on working for a dream, because it could be your way out of misery."

"So finding this pearl lady is a dream now?"

"No, but I have a feeling she is not just 'the pearl lady,' but someone I will know for a long time." Nader went on talking to Leo, who listened carefully while staring at Nader's big brown eyes. "If we give up each purpose we think is impossible to achieve, we would be living life through defeats. Even if the purpose was as silly as maybe returning this pearl, it is a purpose. It is not about the goal to be achieved, it is the path to get there."

Leo reflected on his life, and found himself silently talking to himself: "I once had a dream and gave up on it. Then another dream, and gave up on it, and then another dream. I noticed there was a pattern. My dreams were thoughts that I expressed to my friends and family. Thoughts are powerful, they create realities, but alone they are not enough. Thoughts require our desire to lead a journey, our commitment to the experiences that life brings along, and the luck that we create in life. I always gave up because of my family, and now I need to change the pattern."

Nader handed the papers to Leo, but was lost in his thoughts. He remembered all the times he had to face obstacles in life. Born as a refugee in Kabar, Nader was not allowed access to most civil rights. He lived in refugee camps that were over populated, living in the worst conditions available to human beings.

He did not run away from his misery only, but also from what comes of it. He escaped a past full of war's dust, rich with untold stories that changed lives.

Both Nader and Leo had limits put upon them, the difference between the two being that one had decided to face the circumstances, and the other had allowed the situation to take over. Leo was failing to realize that it was time to cross the line of limits, and be an independent man that his family would eventually be proud of. He still feared sacrifices, and so became a victim of the situation.

Leo decided to focus on the task at hand, and narrowed down the list of events to half, crossing out all events remaining on the list that his grandmother would not attend.

Once again I wanted to talk to Nader and tell him that Leo had just crossed out the event which my

Camilia *was* actually going to attend. It was time for the young man to learn whether to follow what others suggested or what he felt. Until then, Nader himself had not looked carefully at the list he'd printed. I was not surprised that he would not do this. The great thing about observing life from a distance is all the details you get to notice about things and people. I could by now tell that Nader did not pay attention to detail, though I did not judge: often, it is not about what we are, but how we live the character we have chosen to be.

Leo's mobile phone rang, and he became nervous. He excused himself and asked Nader to wait. It was his parents calling to ask why he is late. When fifteen minutes passed by without him returning, Nader decided to keep on with his journey, feeling betrayed by his so-called partner.

He thought, I will wait another five minutes for him; he said he would be right back. Maybe because he is Italian, his two minutes are twenty, just like us Arabs. I have more things to tell him, he seemed sad.

Nader felt an instant and strong connection with Leo, and he felt deep sadness at the thought of continuing his quest without him. Observing your world from here now, I see this happening all the time. Love is not a difficult feeling; it is the process of letting go that brings obstacles and hardships to us. It was Nader's choice to either remain waiting for Leo or to continue on his journey. While we take our time to resolve similar conflicts by deciding on a choice, the universe sometimes acts faster and destiny is reshaped. The latter was Nader's case, and as he spoke his mind aloud, he caught the attention of a girl sitting by his table. "Why is this happening? He would have been a perfect person to help me tonight. He sounded funny and nice."

Amanda, the girl sitting besides Nader in the cafe, was a Master's student at the same university he was in. They had never met, but Amanda overheard Nader speaking and saw him looking upset. She found Nader handsome, which he was, and thought of a creative way to start a conversation with him.

She asked, "Did you also get stood up on a date?"

Nader did not know what to answer, and found himself repeating his story and how he'd met my Camilia. His story caught Amanda's interest, and in fact there were many things about Amanda that caught Nader's. She was a beautiful girl who appealed to Nader as well, creating an atmosphere of attraction and instant lust. She listened carefully to everything he had to say, and asked for every detail about his encounter with Camilia. When he was finished, she said, "The pearl lady will be found, and so will Leo, he might have had an emergency. Let yourself be free and see how the universe comes back for you. What are you focused on right now?"

"Finding the pearl lady."

Amanda said, "Then let's find her and forget about

Leo for now. The pearl lady is the direction of your mission, and Leo is for the universe to decide if you two meet again. Some things in life are predestined, and other things are created by us."

Amanda was trying her best to impress Nader and show him that she was a smart girl. She was assured that she accomplished that when Nader replied, "Wisely said. What do you feel is the best step to take now to find the pearl lady?"

"Well, you said that she drove away in a nice car, so take off any event happening at a venue where nice cars don't park outside. It sounds odd but it might be true." Amanda went through the list of events, those that remained after the elimination done by Riad and Leo. Amanda never looked at the crossed-out events and Nader had still not looked carefully at the events. Thus, both were looking in the wrong place.

At Nader's age, thoughts took time to become reality. I knew he was young, and the beauty of youth is the learning experiences, which shape the adult-to-be. Although he knew that an effort had to be put in when making a dream come true, he was allowing others to choose the destiny of his journey. This usually ends either way, and nothing in life is but a route to another path, another journey.

Nader was following a feeling, and he made of it a dream to fulfill. When fate calls the present we live in, we create paths towards one end: what is meant to be.

Leo had described him as a philosopher, I thought

of him as a learner. I did not mind watching a young man lead a journey and keep me entertained that day, but I did mind how my Camilia was feeling, not far away.

She seemed fine as she ate her dessert, not only thinking about the pearl necklace, but also about Nader. I always knew that she wished to have had a son, but I also knew that it was never too late for her to find one. Things always came together for Camilia because her soul was as beautiful as she was, and such souls only deserve the best.

Nader and Amanda continued looking at the remaining seventeen events, but none of them was the one Camilia was attending.

Amanda said, "You still have two and half hours. Can I help and be with you until you meet the pearl lady?"

Nader smiled. "You are the third to promise me that today."

"Third time's a charm. Let's call these seventeen venues and explain the situation we have. Maybe they can help. Event venues know their patrons."

"I have no phone, do you?"

"No, but you can use the one at my home. I don't live far from here." Amanda's beauty persuaded Nader that he was not wasting time—after all, he was in the company of a gorgeous girl who was offering help.

"Let's hurry then, we have a lot of calls to make." Nader walked with Amanda down the busy street of the island, soon arriving at her apartment.

Only a few blocks away, Camilia and Wahab were leaving their restaurant.

Nader was focused on his quest to find my Camilia, but unfortunately trouble was focused on Nader—and everyone connected with him.

# Chapter Four: The Trouble

I lived my life trying to figure out why things happen the way they do. After that bullet ended all the dreams I had, I learned the lesson through Camilia and was now being reminded of it through Nader. Things happen in life for a reason, but let me explain how I got to master this philosophy thanks to the twenty-four-year-old and his new friend Amanda.

Amanda had been leading a wild life on the island. Her parents lived on a different island in the Atlantic. She had travelled the world with many lovers, and after several failed relationships, she found herself juggling jobs at bars while studying at the university. Although alcohol and drugs were always her way of coping with life, she never allowed that to affect her studies in literature. She was an "A" student, beautiful and smart, but she always ended up behaving in a way society labelled as "bad," or "trouble." She, like the majority of humanity, did not know how to be single. She always wanted someone to be by her side because of issues she'd brought from her past into her present.

Since my death in 1946, I have never understood how our societies were brought to so utterly judge their members. While some governments engage in the most inhumane activities, like war and violence, their citizens are ostracized for habits and choices they make in their own lives. It looks unfair, but a system has to run. If I could speak to some of the decision and policy-makers, I would ask them to go down to the root of the situations that lead youth into addiction and trouble.

Amanda appeared very innocent and naive to Nader, who was once again judging a book by its cover. The cover was a beautiful face, but the book was a troubled life.

Soon they arrived at an old building where students lived on the island. It was run by an Italian couple, Giovanni and Dalida, who looked at Nader and rolled their eyes.

Giovanni said, "She is bringing back another guy, this time still early in the evening."

Dalida countered, "I told you not to rent to her. I never had a good feeling about that girl."

As Giovanni checked out Amanda's petite and toned body, he replied to his wife, "Her lease will come to an end soon, there's not many weeks left for school to be over."

"I have heard this before, over and over again," said Dalida. "Every semester you repeat the same thing since she moved here."

Amanda, clueless, smiled and waved hello to the old couple as she walked up the stairs with Nader.

It was starting to drizzle, and the wind only got stronger when my Camilia and Wahab stopped walking around and entered the same café that Nader had just vacated. They took refuge from the rain, and soon Camilia was sipping a mint tea, which reminded me of the first time we had tea together at a French café. It was a few weeks after we had first met in Saghar.

I'd just arrived back in Paris and was thinking about those grey eyes all the way there. I remember running into the post office first thing so that I could use the phone to speak to Camilia. The same voice answered, and the same light radiated again. I was quick in making plans with her to meet at the local café we'd talked about during the walking tour in Saghar.

I was half an hour early for my one o'clock appointment with the most beautiful woman I had yet seen. I was very excited to meet her, to look at the grey eyes again, and sink into their depths.

And soon there she was, wearing a white embroidered dress that she'd bought at the local market in Saghar, and a hat that matched her black shoes. Elegant and graceful as I remember, she walked in the café and lit up the room with her smile.

We both liked the same music and art, and found ourselves talking about life for hours. It saddens me that I am not able to remember every little thing we discussed, because I was daydreaming most of the five hours we spent together. Later that year, we would spend many similar afternoons, always in a public place, never in private, as Camilia wouldn't accept that until we were married.

I was thirty-nine and had not thought about marriage until then, something my mother never understood when I regularly rejected the girls of Saghar she wanted me to marry. When my mother joined me here in this world, I told her, "You see mother? Everything happens for a reason. Good for some, not as good for others. Life goes on."

These were the words I said to my mother in this world, but she did not understand what I meant, and instead still blamed Camilia for everything that happened. "I told you she was trouble from the beginning, but you did not listen. Do you know what this woman has done to us? Do you see the war between Saghar and Kabar? We also lost you! I spent years crying and the sadness never left me."

I explained to my mother what happened, as Abu Khalil had told me, and that it actually worked out for me to be an observer of life rather than someone engaged in it, as I learned more. My mother just did not understand and it was the last time I would talk to her about it.

Back on the island, Nader entered Amanda's apartment and quickly noticed that it was six o'clock, two hours away from the event. He panicked and could not keep quiet this time. "Are we going to start phoning the venues?"

Amanda smiled. "I want to smoke a joint first."

Nader had smoked hashish before, when he was only fifteen years old. The youths of the refugee camp Nader lived in were starting to get into drugs at that age. They graduated from their schools not to find universities they might study at, or jobs they might get to support their families. Idel refugees in Kabar had been denied rights, living in hard conditions in camps in Kabar. Some believed it was a conspiracy between foreign powers and local authorities to put the drugs in the hands of the youth and ruin their generation, so that they would forever be silent about their lost rights.

Amanda rolled her marijuana as she started phoning the first venue. She waited for a long time, over five minutes, without getting hold of anyone.

"If every phone call is going to take that long," said Nader, "it will be morning before we know it."

Amanda hung up the phone, and thought for a minute as she passed the marijuana cigarette to Nader. He did not want to smoke, but found himself taking a puff, thinking that he should stay focused to find Camilia. Amanda broke the silence with her idea. "We will steal my landlord's car keys and go around all the venues of the island looking for her."

Nader agreed. "Great idea, seems like you have

done it before. We better put this cigarette off and get going." They finished and went down the stairs. Nader watched out for the Italian couple who were surprised that the young man was leaving so early. They giggled as they commented.

Giovanni said, "He did not last long with the beast inside!"

"I can't wait for this beast to leave. No more young girls in here." Dalida was worried about Giovanni, who stared at Amanda every time he saw her. She was jealous, as every woman would be, even though Giovanni could be Amanda's grandfather.

The problems began for Amanda and her landlords when she was seen tanning topless in the backyard of the building. Giovanni, who did not have a problem seeing the topless young girl, had to act as frustrated as his wife was. It was the second day of her stay two years ago, and it definitely did not make a good impression. It was legal to be topless on the island, but not to the conservative and old-fashioned Italian couple. They considered what she did morally unacceptable and detrimental to the reputation of their student home apartments.

Now Amanda, as she had done several times, climbed up the back stairs to the landlords' kitchen. She grabbed the set of keys from the hanger they kept them on and went back down. To distract the couple as the car left the front yard, Amanda broke the water pipe in the back, and made her way to the front of the apartment building where Giovanni and Dalida looked at her from their balcony.

Amanda said, "Giovanni, I was throwing the rubbish in the back and saw that the water pipe is broken again. It's making a huge mess and with the rainstorm coming, you could end up having big problems."

Dalida and Giovanni got up and raced down the stairs that led to the yard. They were always very mindful about their property. Amanda ran to the car and urged Nader to hurry. Nader opened the car window as Amanda started to drive towards the areas highlighted on the map for the remaining events, though none of which was the one my Camilia was going to. Nader looked out the window as he lit his cigarette, and he put the papers on the back seat when Amanda said it would take at least ten minutes to get to the first destination.

The rainstorm had now moved closer to the island, and the wind was blowing stronger than ever that day. The wind made its way into the car and blew away all the papers of the event listings. The two then started an argument, fuelled by Amanda's blaming Nader's carelessness and Nader's defensive response to her anger.

"You should not have put the papers in the back! These are where we are going. Where do we head now? This island is full of events."

Nader was irate. "You know what? Let me out here.

I will find my own way without this attitude I am getting from everyone who is supposedly offering to help find the pearl lady."

Likewise infuriated and insulted, Amanda pulled to the right of the road and Nader got out in the rain, just as he had requested. Now he was once again alone, and only one hour and thirty minutes away from his chance to meet Camilia. It was starting to rain heavier than the drizzles, which made the roads of the island slippery. And now, he was also hungry; it had been hours since he had last eaten.

Amanda drove away in Giovanni's car back to her apartment. When she arrived, Giovanni and Dalida were still busy trying to fix the water pipe in the rain. Amanda felt that she had to do a good deed after breaking the pipe and stealing their car. She went to help the couple, and while it was indeed a good deed for her and Giovanni who did not mind seeing Amanda wet and close to him, Dalida rejected and asked her to go up to her room and leave them alone.

As with Camilia, and me in fact, Nader had left an impact on Amanda. "When someone is this determined to return a pearl, why am I not focused on what matters to me, my life for heaven sakes?" She talked to herself as she looked out the window and saw Giovanni and Dalida focused on their own situation, the broken water pipe. Amanda was now recalling her life as a rebellious teenager who caused trouble in school. She was a good student, which excused her for what she did. She'd started dating boys at a young age, soon went travelling with them, and later found herself back on the island after a painful breakup. She was single now, and had just realized that she had never been alone for any real length of time. But in a few hours, tragedy would allow her to see beyond what she had been so used to in life. Trauma is the enemy that can turn into a friend, causing an emotional clot in our life and then awakening our buried feelings.

I wished again I were able to speak to both Nader and Amanda to tell them how I was learning that everything was happening for a reason. Had the wind not blown the papers out of the car, the two would have found themselves looking for Camilia in the wrong places, and would have not found her. Now it was up to Nader and his journey to know whether the pearl would ever get back to the eleven other ones and open the safe.

And what had Camilia written down that afternoon after she had bought the safe?

It was in 1946, a few days after my murder. Camilia sat down with her newly bought safe and put in it a picture of me, along with her journal and a piece of paper. In her journal, she always talked about her days, feelings and thoughts. I never read except what she shared. We would go to cafés in Paris and stay for the whole day talking, and sometimes she would read parts of her journal. She called it "The Confessions Box" because she always repeated: "Honesty begins between us and ourselves, and then it will show to others without much effort from us. It becomes our nature."

When the safe was locked, Camilia became relieved and was then able to gather herself. A year after, she asked everyone she knew for help. She had made powerful contacts through her job as a translator to a company that had many influential clients. They all agreed to help my Camilia get her rights to own my production plants but failed to succeed in face of the war and corruption in Saghar.

That bullet was fired a few minutes after the Sheikh had made Camilia my wife. I was waiting for the ceremony to end, so that I could take her home and make love to her. Camilia and I had only made love once, the night before our wedding, in a tent in the desert. It was her wish after two years of waiting, and it was my absolute joy. It was magic created by two souls that loved one another, and were meant to be eternally together, which indeed became the case.

All these years, I wanted to live in Camilia's heart. When I felt her pain, I made her feel better with my love. When I felt her fear, I hugged her heart tight to bring her peace. I did not interfere with her life, because love only lives in the heart.

Thus Camilia was now in the car making her way to the event, trying to get there an hour before the show to enjoy a glass of wine at the nearby bar with Wahab. Since he'd met Camilia in 1987, Wahab had never left her. I don't know if the two were ever romantically involved; these things I tried to avoid knowing. It would have hurt me to see my Camilia with another man.

But let me put it this way: he was a very good friend who visited Camilia all the time in Europe and later on the island. He was a businessman who had (and this I know for sure) affairs in the countries he visited. I checked on him regularly, because I cared for all those who loved my Camilia. He was very well dressed and for his age, he kept a very good appearance. He always played sports and never worried about life.

He was the master of the philosophy that everything happens for a reason. And he was sure that the reason was always occurring for *his* purposes and interests. This is why he did not have many wrinkles on his face and the ladies loved him. Still, if I was alive, I would have looked as good as he did, if not better. I would have been the only man Camilia looked at every morning. Alas, life did not want this to happen. I understand.

Wahab had spoken to many people about his secret for happiness: detaching oneself from one's past. He never spoke to Camilia about his past, and always avoided the subject. She only knew that he was from Saghar, and that he did not wish to settle down. He loved having Italy as his home, and enjoyed travelling all year around. He treasured his freedom, and he wished to continue living that way. He did not care much about talking to Camilia about her past; he always talked about the present moment, and never missed a chance to flirt with her.

Camilia and Wahab arrived at the bar, and were sitting by the window watching the rain. It was a romantic scene that I loved observing, and with a sigh, I confess that I would have preferred if I were there instead of Wahab.

Camilia said, "The speakers at the event have travelled from their war-torn countries to speak to us today. There will also be musicians."

"I'm sure you've chosen the best entertainment, as always. Do you still listen all the time to Maria Callas?"

"Of course! Beethoven too. I haven't changed, young man, didn't you say that earlier?"

"I did. And you aren't asking about the pearl anymore, thank goodness."

"Didn't you also tell me to wait until the event is over before to worry again?"

Wahab laughed and tapped his temple. "That's right, I did—see, I am not that young anymore."

Across town, time was racing and so was Nader's heartbeat. There was little time left before he would have to think of other ways to find my Camilia. First he stopped at a restaurant to get a bite to eat. He was trying to finish his cigarette before making his way in when a blond tall man, Richard, walked by. They exchanged smiles and made their way inside.

Nader and Richard were both wet from the rain,

and were greeted and seated by Maria, the waitress, at tables close to one another.

Nader never liked potatoes, but loved cheese. The blond Australian fellow was exactly the opposite. He loved potatoes but never ate cheese. Maria went to Nader first. "What can I get for you?"

Nader said, "An omelette, with no potatoes and extra cheese, and some coffee too, please. I am in a bit of a rush."

Maria nodded. "We all are, my friend, and I will get your order in fast."

Maria then turned to Richard's table. "And you, sir?"

Richard, who had been eavesdropping, said, "I will have the same, but with extra potatoes and no cheese."

Maria then looked at them both and said, "You two should be friends, you won't fight over food."

And so Nader and Richard had a good laugh and started a conversation. Soon Nader found himself telling his story once again to another stranger. This time he was comforted by Richard's smile and friendly personality.

A few years ago, Richard had moved to the island from Australia to work as a carpenter. He was sweet and liked by everyone. He had just broken up with his girlfriend and was getting used to dining alone. He was moved by Nader's story, but did not have a clue about how to help. He encouraged Nader to enjoy his meal and coffee, turn the pearl in to the police, and wait for destiny to make the final decision.

But then he said, "I am free now and can help you. I have a small car I can take you around with. That's everything I can do for you."

Nader sighed. "Another car, another offer of help."

"Excuse me?"

"Thank you, I will come with you. I have a feeling I will find her. If it is eight o'clock and I haven't, we will turn in the pearl."

Richard saw Maria coming. "Your meal is here, please eat, and don't wait for mine."

There wasn't much time left before the event, and Nader was starting to lose hope. I realize now that it is when people are close to losing hope that they move faster in the direction of the target. They let go of fears because they get the sense that they have nothing to lose. The two ate their meals quickly and left the restaurant, with an hour to go before the event. They walked under an umbrella as the rain grew heavier.

I would have breathed a sigh of relief when I saw them leave the restaurant in the direction of the venue, the Moroccan Cultural Centre, a five minute walk away. It was one of the places Richard had thought about.

But my joy did not last long as I took a look at the table where Nader had been sitting and saw a sparkle there on the table. I wanted to take another look, but soon Maria had already cleared the tables. I was frightened, as it seemed like the shiny pearl had been thrown with the leftovers but I couldn't be certain.

Still I knew that if it had, it would be happening for a reason. Except that I was now unsure as to what this reason might be. I was sure that Nader was finally in the right direction towards the event. I knew he took the pearl out at the restaurant and had shown it to Richard, but I wasn't sure if he took it with him. I was very curious and took a look at his hand where he kept it. It was not there anymore. He had been distracted by the young man's funny accent and stories, and did not notice the absence of the pearl.

They walked along the wet streets of the island, under the rain, with Richard's umbrella covering the two of them as they shared stories about life, war, and the experiences they each had been through. They headed to Richard's nearby house to pick up the car and continue the journey. What Nader and Richard did not know then was something very major they had in common.

Yes, we all travel the roads of life with smiles, hiding what some see as secrets, others as experiences, and a few as untold stories which one day are finally revealed as confessions.

# Chapter Five: The Mystery

When I look back now, I understand the role that each person played in my life. Experiences are the events that we live, and people are the actors of the situations we encounter. We each play a role and move destiny in the direction that our interactions and feelings lead us toward. Some people's roles remain mysterious—until you come to my world.

When Nader showed up in Camilia's life, I was all set to follow his journey. I made this choice because I had a good feeling about it. The privilege of being in the World of the Dead is the ability to access information about the past. The past here is not as important as the future, and it should be that way in your world. In the World of the Dead, the past only feeds our curiosity. We choose what parts of it to look at, because we know that the less we carry from it, the lighter our baggage is, so the easier the road towards the future will be. With Camilia, my choice has always been to choose the best moments of the past to remember. With Nader, my curiosity of discovering more about him allowed me to dig deeper.

Quite a few years before Nader moved to the island, he'd gotten into some trouble back in his home country. He was fourteen when he joined a local group that promoted nationalism to support Kabar in the war, and offered refugees protection alongside values he had been brought up to believe in. He was approached by a teacher who recruited youth to the organization in the school he attended. Many organizations had been formed since my death as a response to war. Some of them did great work, while others used the vulnerable for their own benefits.

The first year, Nader attended weekly meetings where he learned about the activities of the organization. They held events to raise awareness about the importance of improving the lives of refugees in camps, organized demonstrations around the country to get the politicians' and organizations' attention, and raised money when required. They also helped protect the border with Saghar and when needed, they provided people to volunteer in the military. There had been many violent fights between Saghar and Kabar, and the military required the assistance from the organization.

Nader soon became one of the brightest members of the organization, well known for leading student protests calling for the rights of his people, and thus a great fundraiser for the group. He was a popular student, and his fellow friends followed his ideas and plans. But the higher leaders of the organization, who were a mystery and whom none of the students had ever seen, noticed a bigger potential in the fifteen-year-old. Besides the activism, Nader was a bright student who was liked by everyone. He also had a friend whom he was very close to, and who later became another member in the organization.

Samir was a few years older than Nader, and he joined the organization not out of interest but out of curiosity about what his close friend was part of. He was very protective of Nader and decided to join to keep an eye on him. Samir thought that the structure of the organization was mysterious, as many of his questions were not answered by the few adolescents who ran the focus groups, classes and protest-organizing sessions. Samir advised Nader to quit and focus on his high school studies, as the two planned to leave together for Europe after his graduation. But Nader never listened, and the enthusiasm of his youth took him down a dark road.

Things did not go as planned, and Samir's curiosity turned into a dangerous game that he and Nader played, and later paid with consequences that changed their destinies. Nader was not the only one playing games. At the same time, miles away in Australia, Richard also found himself toying with danger and harm.

Richard was a bright fellow who excelled in

information and technology. He lived in a poor Australian suburb where he was known to his neighbours to be remarkable at what he did. His friend Ali always asked his help with little projects. Ali would also invite Richard for get-togethers with his friends. But Ali's friends were part of a group that was planning an attack on the capital. They were recruiting men to plan and implement the operation. Richard was the perfect fit for such a purpose: he was a "Westerner" capable of programming and detonating a bomb without raising suspicions. The masterminds behind the organization that Ali belonged to tempted the young Australian fellow, showering him with gifts, money, girls and parties.

Eventually, Ali's friends asked Richard to visit the warehouse from which they operated. They attended regular meetings, planning attacks in various cities, but had not yet implemented any.

It was a Saturday evening when Richard arrived at the warehouse, wearing his grey trousers and a tucked-in white shirt. The guard at the door asked him to remove his hat and to empty his pockets.

Richard resisted. "I am only here to see Ali, Muhammad, Issam, and Zein."

The guard frowned. "Do I have to repeat what I said?"

Richard had always lived a simple life in the suburbs of the Australian capital. His parents worked as teachers; he was a carpenter's apprentice and also a student in computer programming. He had two older brothers who always took care of him. The guard frightened Richard with his tone of voice, serious expression, and authoritative speech. Richard was starting to debate whether he should get out of the old abandoned warehouse when the situation was saved by Ali. "Anything wrong here? Welcome, Richard."

The guard interrupted. "He doesn't want to empty his pockets. You know the rules."

Ali smiled. "It's OK. It's Richard's first time here. Let him in this time." Ali approached Richard, put his arms around his back and walked with him into the building. The first floor was empty but for a few tables, chairs and smoking pipes set in some of the corners. A set of playing cards had been thrown on the floor. Ali walked Richard to the back of the first floor, explaining that this was an entertainment space for the organization's members.

Richard, still innocent and slow on the uptake, said "What organization?"

Ali explained. "You know, my youngest brother died back home when an Australian soldier shot him, fearing that the sixteen-year-old may be a suicide bomber. He killed him."

Richard felt worried and said, "I am sorry to hear this, but what does it have to do with the organization and this place?"

Ali explained, "If someone came into your house and killed your brother and raped your mother, wouldn't you want my help to seek revenge?"

"I wouldn't be silent, that's for sure."

"Exactly, brother, this organization is for people like me, who want to seek revenge."

"And what do I have to do with this?" asked Richard.

"You are my friend, aren't you?" Ali walked Richard into the back, up a staircase that led to a shed attached to the warehouse, and to the second floor. There, a group of familiar faces were gathered around a table, looking at the map of the Australian capital. Issam was smoking a cigarette; he put it out and gave Richard a hug. "Here comes the computer genius now."

Richard blushed. "Who? Me?"

Issam explained, "Listen my friend, we have been taking care of you, and now I have no other person to ask this favour from. Basically, the government here is backing the war at home, and we want to send a message to them."

Richard chewed a fingernail. "What kind of message?"

Issam chuckled. "You ask too many questions, now be patient and listen. Are you hungry? Fancy a beer?"

"Can we finish talking about your favour first?"

Issam's smile turned dark. "What did I say? Too many questions get you in too many troubles. Curiosity is the tool handed only by the strongest. Are you a strong man?"

Zein said, "Muhammad, get up and get a few beers

for Richard. Get some snacks on your way too."

Richard wished he was dreaming then. This was a nightmare he was waiting to wake up from. He was looking at the people around him with fear, feeling the anger and revenge they sought. He was learning about a new face of humanity, the hurt face, the one that seeks revenge.

Richard's upbringing had been simple compared to the group he was with. While his main worries as a child were focused on innocent matters like what Santa was going to bring him, Ali and his friends were war children who lived in conflict and violence. War doesn't only leave wrecked towns and homes, it destroys minds and wounds hearts. Violence is often the reflection of itself, and terrorism becomes the manifestation of anger in its victims.

Richard recalled the earlier conversation he had with Ali, trying to find a way to understand the desire of violence his friend had. He would not be able to understand yet, because only those who lived war can explain the damages it leaves upon their behaviours. I always wished that there was more aid for psychological assistance to war victims than there are now. War damages are beyond what is seen in newspapers and on television. They can only be explained by the stories of people who lived through it.

The time passed by, Richard in his thoughts, Ali on his phone, and Issam preparing documents to share with Richard. At last he said, "We have a bomb that will be put in a mail package delivered to a politician. We want a program that remotely detonates the bomb without tracking the source. Ali mentioned you are talented."

Richard asked, "And who is the politician?"

Issam showed Richard a picture of the target, explaining that the operation would be taking place in her public office.

"But what about the innocents in the building? What about her family? What you are talking about is huge destruction, Issam."

Issam shrugged. "What about the innocents they decided to kill supporting wars back in our home countries? An eye for an eye."

Richard countered, "Then the world will have no eyes left to see its beauty."

Issam scoffed. "Don't be poetic with us now. I need you for a favour, nothing more. You do it, or give me back all that money I have been giving you."

Richard was known to turn red when he was angry or nervous. This time, it was both. He was defeated by these friendships he had always found somewhat mysterious. He was nervous because he was stuck in a situation where he could not pay back what he had been given, nor could he hurt his nation. His few years at university had taught him some phrases that he found himself sharing in a trembling voice. "There are other ways to send messages. Why destroy the lives of innocent people—or my life, for that matter?"

Issam said, "Your life will be fine. You carry out the operation, take your money and get on a plane out of here. You are a world traveller, and people like you don't belong to one place anyway. "

"And my family?"

Issam laughed once more. "You ask too many questions. Do I take this as a yes?"

Richard said. "I need some time to think."

"Fine, take your time, but this has to happen before the electoral campaign next month. And if you don't want to return this favour, have the money ready. It's pay back time, or one of your family members will be the price tag."

Richard froze, but spoke with a confidence he did not have. "No need for this talk, mate, your favour will be returned."

"Then do I take this as a yes?"

"Yes."

Now destiny had Nader and Richard walking together on one of the island's streets, talking about everything they enjoyed, hiding the dangerous games that each had played in their own ways.

At the same time the two fellows of mystery walked side by side, my Camilia walked by Wahab's side. It was 7:00 p.m., and the two were still at the nearby bar. The wind was blowing softer but the rain had started heavier. Nature had not yet made up its mind, neither about the rain, nor about the destiny of the pearl.

Camilia began, "Maybe it is time to tell you more about the pearls."

"Twenty-five years later? I'd say it's time. I've seen these pearls every time I've seen you, each and every time. Today I see them around your neck, and with one missing, they still look good."

"Of course, they look good, he gave them to me."

"Your husband, whom I look like."

"Yes, him. He put them around my neck before our wedding and after he died, I made them into a lock for the safe I always carry around, the one by the armchair in the library."

"The one you were about to throw in the sea when we first met?"

"That's right, the same safe."

"Well, what's in it?" Wahab asked softly, for he knew this was a sensitive topic for Camilia.

Camilia paused before saying, "My journal up to the day he was killed and something I had always wanted to tell him, but never got the time."

"What kind of thing? Anything I need to know? What is inside the safe, Camilia? Anything you know that could have given more answers about his murder?"

Camilia gave a weak smile and said, "The truth is like oil in water, it always surfaces."

Wahab sighed. "After sixty-six years, there is no more water or oil, they've evaporated."

"But the truth doesn't rise on its own; we have to

keep checking the oil and water. I've checked and renewed them for sixty-six years now, never gave up."

"You, giving up? These don't go hand in hand. I don't like to talk about your past, but I know that the war between Saghar and Kabar is based on more than the people need to understand. If your secret helps that, then it should not be a secret."

Camilia ordered another drink and changed the subject of the conversation to talk about the event they were about to attend. "It's a few speakers talking about being refugees, artists from war-torn countries, and art from around the world. This is going to be a perfect evening."

My Camilia always had strong intuitions, but she did not in fact know that she was about to have one of the greatest evenings of her life. There were many things Camilia did not know. For example, a few months before this day, the government of the island had launched an investigation about her.

I'd visited the Criminal Investigation Unit's office, down by the southern port of the island. A few men had gathered around the table, looking at the wealth Camilia had brought and transferred into the island. The government was worried about her being involved in money laundering, which I am confident to tell you that she was not.

Lia Adams was the junior officer who was new to the Department. Her first assignment was to find out everything about Camilia: her wealth, relationships and whatever she might know. Lia's research led to just one result: here was an old woman who'd fought for years to get the rights to her deceased husband's businesses and production plants. A few days before the event in question, Lia had begun watching Camilia's house closely, looking for visitors and guests.

Until earlier this afternoon when Nader showed up, Lia's assignment was starting to feel boring. She had seen no one come to visit Camilia. She knew of Wahab, and his background check results showed nothing but an Italian who was a successful businessman and an old friend of Camilia.

Lia was a few meters away from Nader that afternoon when she saw him approaching Camilia's house and walk past it. Her curiosity was triggered further when she saw Nader and Camilia talking briefly by the car. And so all that afternoon Lia followed Nader, trying to understand his relationship with my Camilia. His random discussions with different strangers confused her, but when he later met Richard, she grew worried. Richard had been flagged previously, and his history was very well known to authorities.

When Lia saw Nader coming in Richard's car, she was worried even more. Her suspicions were now scattered, trying to draw a relationship between Camilia, Nader and Richard. She watched the two carefully and shadowed them in her own car.

Richard and Nader were following a map, looking for my Camilia.

Richard said, "Why don't you just stay on the island after your classes?"

Nader sighed. "Maybe, now let us stay focused on finding the pearl lady."

"You know that the pearl is probably not the most expensive thing this lady owns."

"Maybe so, but she still has to have it."

"Why?" Richard made a left turn and glanced at his new friend, worried.

"Actually it is not about the pearl. It is about the purpose. I have in mind that I need to find her and I have a feeling it is for something big. I grew up as a refugee, and the best thing about that is our attachment to any purpose, small or big." As he was speaking about the pearl, Nader then realized that it was no longer in his hands. He panicked once again, blaming himself for wasting time with people when he could have taken the pearl to the police station. "Why did I do this? Why?"

Richard stopped the car to look up the number of the restaurant and phone them, and as Maria hunted around, Nader started pacing near the car now parked on the side of the road. Lia watched the scene, more confused than ever before. She was now worried that the three, Camilia included, were organizing some sort of activity that could lead to an attack on the island.

Richard broke the silence. "Maria cannot find the pearl. Did you check your pockets?"

"I did. I checked my pockets. I checked the car."

"So you have lost it?"

Nader began talking to himself as Richard leaned on the car, his back to his newly made friend who was wandering around, thinking what his next move would be. "Don't give up Nader, don't give up. The pearl is somewhere, and the lady is elsewhere. There's forty-five minutes left to find the lady first, then the pearl."

Richard and Lia both heard Nader speaking.

Richard said, "What? You believe in magic now? Just give up, and let's hit a close by bar."

Nader continued to pace. "No, I am not giving up."

"So then what are we now looking for? A lady whose pearl is lost? You want to apologize for losing this all-important pearl?"

"Yes, I am now looking for the two in forty-five minutes, the pearl and her."

Richard sneered. "Well, I am leaving you here then. I'd rather be at a bar when the rainstorm hits. Good luck, mate, and after you are done with your treasure hunt, come to the student party tonight. I might be there, or find me on Facebook: Richard Thompson."

Nader said "Thank you for helping me, well… for trying to help me."

"Good luck, my friend."

He was nice to leave Nader his umbrella, which I thought was sweet. Richard made his way back to the car, and drove away from the street leaving Nader, once again, alone. But in fact, Nader had never been alone along his journey so far. Besides me, there was Lia, who had been watching him from a distance.

Now though, she decided to approach the young man standing in the rain under the umbrella with a cigarette in his mouth. "Smoking is bad for you."

"I know, but it is not the only thing that kills you."

Lia said, "What else kills you?"

"Staying under the rain also kills you", he hesitatingly answered.

She was trying to start a conversation with Nader, but due to his recent experiences, having been left by all those whom he thought were going to help him, he made all his answers short, and excused himself. However, Lia was not the type to give up, like Nader and Camilia. She gathered from Nader that he was an international student on the island, and that he was looking for a woman. Lia then felt she had no other option but to come up with a story as to why she needed to ask the young man a few more questions. "My name is Lia Adams and I work for the island's Police Department. I have been watching you all day as part of a security routine and saw you speak to a few citizens of the island."

Nader was always nervous speaking to the police, even more so now, with forty-five minutes to go. He did not like this lady showing her officer badge. Nader uttered a few words, explaining his story to Lia who was amused by what she heard, and at the same time relieved that it was not what she'd thought. Lia was trained to know when someone was lying and when she heard Nader speaking, she sensed integrity and the truth.

She had been listening to Camilia's phone calls and knew from a call with Wahab earlier where she would be. She did not know where Nader lost his pearl, and even I was uncertain where it was now. Again, in the World of the Dead, we choose what to know. While the past is easy to recover for us, the future is a choice. Most of the people in the World of the Dead realize that it is the journey of getting somewhere that matters, so we choose to enjoy the path towards a goal. I have always preferred to know the future through the path towards it, because the joy of a journey is in the experiences that create it.

Being challenged, as she was taking on her first assignment, Lia knew that taking chances was her only way of finding out more about the case. She decided to use Nader and help him at the same time. She wasn't concerned about the pearl, just about Camilia. Now she had a way to reach her target. Lia looked at Nader's face, smiled and said, "As a member of the island's police, I can find out easily who this lady you are talking about is, and where she would be. But I have a favour to ask you."

"Anything. I want to find this lady first, and then search for her pearl in all the places I went to today."

"Don't you want to know first what the favour is?"

"Well, you won't ask me to do anything illegal; you are the police after all. So, anything."

I wished I could tell Nader to never make a promise before knowing what the commitment is.

Lia began, "As far as I know, her name is Camilia Vidal, and she has been on this island for ten years, but never interacted with anyone around. She must be hiding something and you are going to help me with that."

Nader was surprised and also excited. "How do you know who I am looking for?"

"Because I saw you speak to her this afternoon."

"So where is she?"

"We will first agree on the rules, and then I will show you the way."

"Now there are only forty minutes left before her event begins, though."

Lia smiled. "I know."

"But how do you know?"

"I told you, I know *everything*. Now would you let me explain what your mission will be?"

So Lia and Nader sat on a set of stairs starting a conversation that would change Nader's life, Camilia's life, and even Lia's life. Nader was once again getting into a game that would reshape his destiny, but this time very different from the game he'd been involved with in his home town of Kabar.

# Chapter Six: The Confusion

Lia was a complex girl who turned her intelligence and beauty into excellence at her job. She wanted to be a lawyer, and when she graduated from high school she was accepted into most universities to which she had applied.

As the high school student was getting ready for her first year at university, she fell in love with a man a few years older than her. She decided to stand up to her family to be with him, fighting for the love that many people saw inappropriate, because of her age and his.

What is it with people putting a number on sacred emotions like love? I have to say this, because my Camilia faced the same objections when she decided to marry me. Years only count when they are not lived properly, but when we live them with happiness and joy, they are just experiences, not years. This is the secret to remaining young through the decades we get to live.

Lia's parents were both conservative immigrants to

the island, but had lived there for years. They treasured their traditions and values from back home and brought them to the island, influencing the upbringing of their two children, Lia and Roni. Lia soon moved out of her parent's house to live with friends at age sixteen, because of the differences between her views on life and theirs.

Her life was going as planned, until a few weeks before she was about to start her first year of university, when she found out she was pregnant. Sex before marriage was a taboo in the culture of her parents. She thought she would find comfort and peace when reporting the situation to her lover, but found herself mistaken. He confessed that he'd only thought of their relationship as an affair, as he was about to get married to a woman his family thought of as the perfect match for him. So he left Lia alone on her own journey, together with a child that was now living inside her. Lia did not dare to tell the truth to her family, and chose to have an abortion.

But what happened then is that Lia did not only abort a child, she also lost part of herself. She transformed from a nice and sweet girl into what people called a "bitch," and a "mean and insensible" person. She then decided to switch to criminal investigation studies, because she thought that becoming a police officer might give her power and authority after her confidence had been shaken by her so-called lover.

Now Lia did not joke around, was serious all the time, and did not trust any man enough to be in a relationship again. Men always flirted with her, but she did not welcome anyone into her life. She was soon desired by even more men because, as I know from having been one myself, we men always desire a little bit more that which we cannot have.

This may explain my eternal love for Camilia. She too was a woman I could not have. First of all, she was from a different religion. But I also never understood, even after my death, why people make their beliefs their main cause of conflict. If humanity respected all beliefs, there would be no war, no violence. But I digress. Second, Camilia was from a different culture. My parents further disagreed because they wanted me to marry someone from Saghar or the neighbouring Arabic Desert areas. The age difference was not an issue for my parents, as they always wanted me to marry someone younger, believing she could give birth to more of my children. Little did they know that my life would not really matter after forty-one, because I would not live beyond that. I always thought there was plenty of time in life to do what's desired. I did not know that time can compete with us, and actually win the race. In my case, it did.

Camilia was thinking about the pearl again, and she found herself crying, which caught Wahab's attention.

"Look," he said, "we'll report it missing right after the event."

Camilia replied, "But now it's not the pearl that is missing, it is that young man that I think might found it."

Wahab mocked once again, "He's probably a thief, then."

"No you are not getting my point. His big brown eyes spoke to me. They had a story to tell."

"Camilia, we *all* have a story to tell."

"But his is a story I think I want to hear. Untold stories are usually kept in the eyes, and his needed to be shared."

Wahab then looked at Camilia's bright grey eyes. Since he'd met her twenty-five years ago, they saw each other once a year wherever life brought them together. But he knew little about my Camilia. Their conversations were always about art and culture, events they were attending, or new artists that they both liked. Now he could not keep silent as Camilia sipped on her red wine.

"And what is your untold story?"

"Excuse me?"

Wahab leaned closer. "Your eyes also show an untold story. What is it?"

"You mean the pearl?"

"The blasted pearl again. I am asking about your untold story, *not* the pearl."

Camilia leaned back as he moved closer. "Well my pearl is my untold story for now. If I find it, I'll tell my story.

"And if not?"

"Well, some stories are meant to remain untold, they were made only for one person, and other stories were made for all."

"Is there such thing as a story only made for one?"

Camilia smiled. "It is then called a secret, and telling it becomes a confession."

Wahab said, "You are speaking in symbols my dear, is there anything you want to tell? Or confess?"

"I will tell you one thing: we are going to be late for the event, and I like arriving early there. Finish your drink."

Wahab grinned. "As you say, lady."

While the two waited to finish their drinks, and later for the bill to arrive, silence filled the atmosphere. We were all silent, especially of course, *me*. The only place I could not travel into was Camilia's mind, for I was trapped in her heart. I can tell you nothing about what she was thinking, but through her heart, I knew what she was feeling. I can also assure you, and you would agree with me, that she always looked beautiful. This evening she wore a dark grey dress and a hat adorned with a purple bow. The pearl necklace was missing a pearl, but it still looked as elegant as it always did on my Camilia.

Now Wahab was as curious as I was. Funnily enough, we were both thinking the same things. We wondered what Camilia meant by saying that the pearl was her untold story, and more importantly, what that story was.

Few seconds after my death, I did not realize what happened, and was lost in so many thoughts. I looked for Camilia immediately and found her: she was clearly devastated and destroyed because of my murder, angry at my family who blamed her for being the reason that Kabar sent someone to kill me. History is written by people, and many stories were told about the start of that war. The people of Kabar had expressed concerns about a noble, myself, marrying a foreigner and mixing bloods. I know where it all started, and I know how it was ignited with passion and grief. I recall crying out as loud as I could (or rather, couldn't) to stop my mother from hurting my Camilia only a few minutes after my murder.

My mother was saying, "Someone was as angry at him as we were, and wanted him dead better than alive with a foreigner like you."

Camilia wept and said, "Your son is my husband, I love him with all my soul."

"And what did you do to him with your love? Brought him nothing but death. They killed him."

My parents were angry, and it was their way of expressing their feelings of devastation. The guests at our wedding were the same people who carried my body back to Saghar. Everyone was angry, and the few voiced doubts that people from Kabar killed me became the fire that started a long war between the two towns.

Now I was silent again, watching Nader who was

just a block away from where Camilia and Wahab were, and who was at a loss for words. He found himself once again facing an offer from an unknown person, this time realizing that he had to stop playing games.

Lia was the only loud one then; her tone of voice was subdued, but not her demands. She said, "I know where Camilia is, exactly. Now I want you to listen to me carefully. I will get you a pearl; you will take it to her and say it is the lost one. She will be thrilled that you have found it, and will wear the necklace around her neck; she will not notice the difference. Get into her life, make friends with her. I will see you regularly, and each time I will have questions for you to find answers for."

Here Nader was presented with an offer that he did not feel comfortable with. Several years before he moved to the island, the group he belonged to had proposed a different mission. He was asked to travel, pretending to be part of a family, all with forged documents. Their minivan would be transporting what seemed to be their belongings. Their story was they were moving from Kabar to Orden, a town a few miles away. In fact, the alleged family was commissioned to transport weapons and drugs to a group in Saghar in exchange for money for the organization's operations and, of course, the pockets of a few of its leaders.

Nader was starting to understand the industry of

war. The same organizations that fought Saghar, and partook in the war, were providing weapons to the other parties, in exchange for money. Nader realized an equation that took me years to understand: War is money, and money can easily make war.

Back then, Nader accepted the offer as he was under pressure; his family and close friends, like Samir, were being threatened. The weapons were to be transported to another group in Saghar, and the money was to be brought back into Kabar. The mission did not go as planned, and life took Nader in a path he did not expect, ending on the island.

For the past months on the island, Nader's schedule was not merely going to classes and having fun. There was fear chasing him, for he was scared of returning back to Kabar. Now he gathered his confidence, broke the silence and said, "I will help you, but I need help too. I need to stay on the island after my program is over. I need a work permit or residency here."

Lia was trained to sense untold stories, but she knew that she did not have much time to get the story out of Nader. And she wanted to keep going with her mission. "I will help you stay as a citizen of this island; you help me with my mission. Do we have a deal?"

Nader smiled. "We do. We definitely do. Where is Camilia?"

"But if you don't help me with this mission, you will be deported the second I decided. Understood?"

Nader nodded. "Definitely understood. Now,

where is Camilia?"

As far as Lia knew and researched, the event Camilia was attending that night brought refugees from around the world to speak about their experiences growing up in war-torn countries. The event would also have two musical performances: one by a well-known troupe of refugees, and another by a local band from the island. Lia had little time to provide Nader with training and equipment to record any conversation he would be having with Camilia. She said, "The event she is going to is a few minutes away. It is sold out, I know that. You will enter from the back door and meet Sandra, the event coordinator. One of the guest speakers could not make it today; you will tell her your name is Rami Fayat."

"Rami Fayat, that will be me tonight. But do I have to speak?"

"You probably do. I overheard your conversation with Riad, the fellow you met at the internet café. You, as a refugee, can say few moving words that the crowd would appreciate listening to."

Nader was again startled. "How do you know Riad?"

"It's not the time for me to be telling you stories, only instructions for the next few days." Lia did not tell Nader that all the activists on the island were under surveillance. The authorities of the island had been very careful with citizens having a traumatic past. A big part of the island's budget was allocated for the wellbeing of its citizens. A few years ago, a gunman had walked into a restaurant and shot many people. It was an unusual event to occur on this peaceful island. After thorough research, the gunman was discovered to be a troubled young man, and the incident could have been avoided if the authorities of the island had provided psychological assistance to him. Besides an immediate ban of guns, it was then that the island started screening every person who was becoming a citizen. Lia knew that Riad had lost a brother in violence, and his activism may have been a way of venting—or something worse. Thus they kept him under surveillance.

Anxious now, Nader continued, "I am all ears."

"Basically, you will meet with Camilia and give her the pearl back."

"The fake pearl, you mean?"

"As far as we are concerned now, it is the pearl she has been missing. If she invites you for a coffee, lunch or dinner, accept. If not, invite her. I will take care of the bill."

Nader asked, "What do you want to know about her?"

"There is no time to explain now, I will be seeing you and giving you all sort of explanations and instructions later." Lia walked to her car and picked up a device used to record and transmit live conversations. She provided Nader with it, and showed him how it worked. "You must make sure to start all sorts of conversations with her. I know so very little about her, and I need to know more. I want to know who are her relatives, who is her family, who is she and the organizations she worked for before moving here. We only know her name. You should know that since the murder of her husband sixty-six years ago, she never remarried."

"Why should I know that?"

Lia hesitated. "As a refugee you have lost a few people, I am sure, in your life, haven't you?"

"I have lost a friend, Samir."

"Exactly. See, this is a way to start a conversation. Common loss brings people together faster."

Nader did not feel at peace about bringing the fake pearl to Camilia, but knew that he had no other choice at this point. There was something in the universe drawing him to Camilia's path and journey. He said, "I am sure I will come up with something. Don't worry."

Lia checked her phone, then said, "My colleague is bringing a few pearls here, we will pick the closest to the one you lost."

"What if she recognizes that it is not the missing pearl?"

"We'll worry about it then. You get yourself out of there, and I will give you more instructions."

Nader and Lia waited for her colleague to arrive with a collection of over 50 pearls. It took them a few minutes to choose what they believed to be the closest to the missing one.

In fact, I would never have noticed the difference. I clearly remember when I bought the pearls. I was at the market, rushing to find the necklace that had caught my attention. I knew that it would belong to my Camilia forever, though I did not know that it would be the same necklace that locked away her secret.

It was now 7:45 p.m. and Lia said, "I will leave you now at the door of the event, and you are now Rami Fayat, forget about Nader."

"Understood."

"On stage, talk about being a refugee, but try to catch Camilia's attention, for you want to meet with her after the event."

"And then?"

Lia handed him something small. "Take this, it is an earpiece, put it in your ear and listen to what I say."

Nader did not know if he was being set up by Lia for a different purpose altogether, but when desperate, we look for hope anywhere and trust becomes determination's rival, usually with determination winning at the end.

Lia drove Nader to the Moroccan Cultural Centre, kitty-corner from where Camilia and Wahab had sat and drank wine earlier. They were now taking their seats inside the theatre.

Nader arrived at the backstage door and saw Sandra, the event planner who ran the evening. Sandra was originally from the island, but had been overseas for years. On that night, she was coordinating guest speakers from over fifteen countries, which played in Nader's favour as she could not recognize the speakers' faces. He approached her and said, "My name is Rami Fayat, I am a speaker tonight." Nader gave Sandra the fake ID Lia had provided him with earlier, and Jennifer, Sandra's assistant, took Nader to "his" dressing room. Jennifer explained to Nader that when his number is called, he should make his way to the speaker's lounge.

Jennifer said, "Sandra will be there during the event, and will walk you to the stage when it is your turn. Where are you visiting the island from?"

Nader's mind raced. "I am visiting the island from Palestine."

Jennifer nodded. "So you are the second speaker for the night. Someone will come in to put some makeup on for the video recording of the event, and I will bring Nadia back here to say hello."

Nader did not know who Nadia was and did not feel comfortable asking Jennifer.

Jennifer continued. "Nadia will be thrilled to see you again. She tells us all the time about meeting you during her last visit to Palestine."

Nader was nervous that he would be caught lying and forging the identity of one of the speakers. He bluffed, "I can also see her after the event; I would like to have enough time with her."

Jennifer shook her head before leaving the room with a smile. "You stay here, and I will go get her; there is plenty of time before your turn."

Nader wanted to get in touch with Lia, but his device wasn't working where he was, in a basement with no signal. Still, Lia was able to hear everything Nader said through the recorder in his pocket. Jennifer began hunting down Nadia, one of Rami Fayat's friends who had been looking forward to meeting him.

Rami Fayat was supposed to attend the event but had not gotten his visa on time. I once again wished that the world had no borders, because it hurts me when I see people denied any of their rights, as simple as the right to visit another place in the big world I once belonged to.

Nader was getting nervous, turning red and uttering his sentences aloud again. He was about to be caught, embarrassed, and kicked out of the event. He spoke to himself, again in a loud voice: "I should have just told them the truth."

Nader's thoughts were again overheard, and this time his little quirk would get him into a situation that neither luck nor speech skills could save him from.

# Chapter Seven: The Mission

It is time for a confession: for sixty-six years now, I have been scared to know more about my Camilia's thoughts. I have only been an observer of her mission in life, which I was never clear about in the first place. For decades, she fought to obtain her rights to my estate and finding the identity of my murderer. I did not feel defeated when she gave up on finding out who killed me, for how would she have known in a country of corruption and war? I have always known who killed me; it didn't matter to me any longer. When Abu Khalil told me the entire story, I chose to forget parts of it and only focus on the positives. What mattered is my Camilia, and for my people of Saghar to again be at peace with our neighbours of Kabar.

When I first came to the World of the Dead, I was looking forward to travelling to any part of the world, or to any person for that matter. Here I was not judged by anyone for my thoughts or opinions. I was no longer bound to any limits that a country or society had put upon me. My only important mission was to watch out for Camilia.

Right after my murder, I saw Camilia crying loudly over my body, with blood all over her. I comforted her with a hug she probably felt, but no one saw. I stood up and cleaned the blood on my clothes and ran towards the man who fired the bullet at me after he had remounted his black horse.

I ran faster than the horse until he stopped to drink water at a neighbouring well. He did not see me. His heartbeat was loud; I could hear them as he poured water in his palms and washed his face. He was terrified, and I could swear that I had seen him before during one of my trips to Kabar. I knew he was sent on a mission to kill me, and that was all I knew before I talked to Abu Khalil.

I yelled at my murderer after chasing him: "You. Why did you decide to end my life at the time it was just starting?"

He did not know where the voice came from, but his fear led him to answer: "I don't know who you are. I only knew about you from them." He thought he was speaking to himself, not knowing that I was now part of him in the form of guilt.

"Who sent you to kill me?" I demanded, but our conversation was interrupted by men who came on more black horses, meeting this young fellow, now a murderer, by the well he drank from. I did not care to know more back then, because I wanted to return to my Camilia, who was still on the sand exactly where I was killed, lying over my body.

I was first, like my people of Saghar, outraged at the people of Kabar who I believed had sent my murderer. When the truth was shown to me by Abu Khalil, I understood everything and did not ask for more details. I knew that the worst was coming to Saghar and Kabar, and so it did happen. I felt sorry for the people of both towns. Some world organizations had tried to make peace between Saghar and Kabar, repetitively failing. Mostly because peace is not created, it is retained from our human nature. This happens with dialogue and acceptance. It also happens by revealing the truth, not just the events that people see. War on the other hand is created from violence, conflict, and lies.

Shortly after my murder, the local police of Kabar and Saghar arrived. My mother was whining and in shock, blaming Camilia for my murder. "They killed him because he was mixing bloods", my mother affirmed. My father blamed Kabar because of the reasons my mother said, and that other people agreed as well. He immediately asked my cousins and friends to start gathering with all the weapons available in Saghar. He said, "We will attack them for the murder of my son. An eye for an eye."

My oldest brother had always been close to Camilia. His fascination with the French culture initiated many of their conversations. He helped

Camilia leave for the capital that same night, and a couple of days after, fly back to Paris. His interest in Camilia was one of the very few reasons I liked him. When I was living, I allowed myself to judge him based on what I carried from the past. He had bullied me when we were young, and it was all that I remembered and based my judgment on. But later in the years, I would respect him for helping my Camilia.

My family's mission was revenge. My father's suspicions and blame led to a war between Saghar and Kabar that had not stopped since. A few weeks after my murder, the tension between the two towns mounted. A group from Saghar attacked the home of Kabar's leader, and killed his son as revenge. The two towns fought for years after, and accumulated reasons for conflict and violence. Saghar leaders decided to stop exporting products to Kabar, and the latter retaliated by cutting off the electricity from our town. Little did they both know that all their assumptions were wrong, and blood was shed for fears, false evidence appearing real. The two towns became independent countries in 1949, with a border separating what was once a big home.

A few months after my murder, Camilia had saved up some money from her work as a translator and hired a lawyer to help her gain her rights and find out who killed me. Frederic, the lawyer, a heartbroken widower, was moved and touched by her story. He helped her without getting paid for his time until he died in 1969. It took my Camilia a journey of over five decades and a few lawyers to get what was hers, but thankfully I included in my original will the following: "Camilia, when carrying my last name as my wife, earns all that I own, in estate, money, and businesses." After my brother Ayham showed the real documents in 2002, it only took a few months before Camilia was granted her rights. Sometimes things happen easily, but for the purpose of one's journey, detours occur.

Back on the island, at the Moroccan Cultural Centre, Nader's mission was quite different from Camilia's decades-long obsession. He just wanted to get out of his tricky situation. Jennifer was busy getting Nadia who was a friend of Rami Fayat, and while she did this Nader practiced not letting his fear control the situation, something he remembered learning from his friend Samir.

Samir had always insisted that Nader leave the group he was involved in, as their agenda was getting clearer to the more mature among the two of them. Nader, on the other hand, found himself too deeply involved to just walk away. In order to protect Nader, Samir decided to join the organization and keep an eye on his friend. Soon the organization arranged a mission to transport weapons and drugs from Kabar to Saghar. Nader and Samir were debriefed by one of the organization's leaders one afternoon: "Samir will be driving a van that will have you Nader, and an old couple. Your passports and documents will show that you are a family moving away from Kabar."

Samir had questions to ask, starting with, "What happens on the way back? How do we explain returning to Kabar so fast?"

The organization's leader said, "You bring me to the second part of the mission." He poured coffee for Samir and Nader, then looked out the window overlooking Kabar. He began, "The group you will meet in Saghar will give you money in exchange of the drugs and weapons. This money is what we use for our work, protests, everything. This organization in Saghar also fights their own government; these weapons are not to fight us."

He took another sip of his coffee and went on. "The old man and woman are staying there; someone else will pick them up. Both of you, and the money of course, will come back here to Saghar with new identities, new passports, new everything. You will give us the money, and each of you will get a bonus."

Nader and Samir carried out their first mission successfully, and it was followed by many other similar ones, always transporting drugs and weapons. They always left before sunrise, made their way to the border and bribed the officials with a little money that got them across the border easily. The organization repetitively threatened the two when Samir insisted that he would not do another mission. Meanwhile, Nader and Samir saved up the money they were earning so that they could leave for Europe after Nader had graduated from school.

The missions always went as planned, but a choice Nader made during one trip would change his life and end his friend's.

On the island, Lia was listening to everything happening backstage, and was able to sense Nader's fear through his heavy breathing. Lia's mission was to get as much information as possible about my Camilia. Thus she did not care about Nader who was not able to speak to her due to a bad signal, but she was sure he would be fine.

Nader was getting nervous, and was about to leave the overcrowded area and exit the building when Jennifer returned alone and said, "Nadia will not have time to see you, because she is welcoming the guests. She will see you after you speak. She apologizes and was glad to hear you got the visa and made it. Sandra will come to get you when it is your turn to speak. Good luck."

It was 8:20 p.m. when the event started. Nader could hear the clapping and the voice of the host for the event. "Welcome to an evening to celebrate culture, refugees and hope. Five refugees from around the world have come here today to speak to all of you. They are speaking about their experiences, their thoughts on aid practices, and their dreams that we can hopefully make happen after tonight. Please welcome on stage, our first speaker, Rahman. He was born in Feran, twenty-five years ago, and ran away from a death sentence to be with us. Tonight, he will be speaking about his story that tells us a lesson: a conflict is the harmful expression of differences."

As the slim Rahman made his way on stage and tested the microphone that was acting up, Sandra reminded Nader that he was next. When Nader and Sandra were talking, they were interrupted by the moving story that was being spoken on stage.

"My name is Rahman, and I am twenty-five years old. Eight years ago, I was a teenager like any of your sons and daughters. I liked Superman, video games, and a Lebanese singer named Elissa. This is also the time when I was exploring and discovering the mysterious world of love.

"Feran, which many of you don't know, is a country on the eastern side of the Sahara. Its conservative leadership has led to laws that violate human rights. For example, homosexuals could be sentenced to death. I was seventeen years old, and Omran was eighteen. He was my very special friend. We had met only a few months before the local police broke into our hotel room. We were both arrested for what was considered improper behaviour, and were jailed for the night in a separate cell at the police station.

"Shortly after dawn, I was taken to speak to an officer. A big man with a wrinkled face, broad shoulders and a deep voice, ordered me to sit. He reminded me of the fear I grew up with. He said, 'In a few hours, you will be hung out in front of everyone, for you have upset God.'

"As I had nothing to lose then, and as I knew that death was a few hours away, I replied, 'God doesn't get upset if we express our love. God gets mad when his people fight one another and kill each other. God is upset at humanity now, at you.'

"The officer came closer to me and put his hand on my mouth to stop me from talking. He then took off his belt, and I thought that, like my father did sometimes, he was going to give me few lashes for speaking my mind. He didn't. Instead he dropped his pants and forced me to give him fellatio. I refused, but then he said, 'You will do this, and you will be free. You will come in here, when I ask you, and do this again whenever I want.'

"I wanted to live. We all do. Life is a gift from God and gifts are to be kept precious. I did what he asked, and saved my life. I was released shortly after without my family knowing. Omran on the other hand, I never saw again. Some people claimed he left the country to work overseas. Others assumed he was kidnapped by the neighbouring Saghar or Kabar, who were constantly in conflict.

"But I knew the truth and never spoke. I became convinced that he was killed that night, for I heard him scream, like all the other prisoners who were tortured at Bleish Prison. Over time, I went to see the officer whenever he requested, and was always sexually abused by him. I asked the officer one time after being raped by him if he knew where Omran was. He demanded that I never ask again or mention his name, and said, 'He obtained a visa from a foreign country and then left you.'

"Until today, I don't know where Omran is. When the officer started to threaten me continuously, I went to the Embassy of this island and applied for refugee status.

"I became a refugee. Displaced from my country, not because of an earthquake or war, but because there was a part of me that I was exploring.

"Today, I speak for an organization that brings people with similar stories here to the island to live in peace where everyone is accepted for who they are, not who they are supposed to be. Thank you." People then clapped for Rahman, whose eyes were filled with tears.

(I wished I were able to speak to him and let him know that Omran was still alive, that he had been transferred to a prison in a neighbouring country as part of a prisoner's exchange agreement. However, Omran and Rahman would later agree that it is these unknowns that become our experiences, and this makes the journey we live in life. I also knew that a few years from now, Rahman would become an advocate for his cause, and eventually he would find Omran after years of waiting. Rahman's experience had defined his purpose, and one day he would get through his journey to the place he always belonged: his loyal love to Omran.)

It was now Nader's turn to take the stage, impersonating Rami of whom he had very little knowledge about. As Nader made his way to the stage, he was shivering. He started getting the signal and could now hear Lia saying, "This is your moment. I did not expect this to happen tonight, I am going to trust you and as I said, I will help you stay on the island."

Nader couldn't care less about what he heard; he was focused of what he already knew. He was finally going to meet my Camilia, and once again, he would be breaking the rules.

Last time he did so was on the way back from one of the missions he and Samir were sent upon. Samir drove the van back to Kabar as a mother and her child slept in the back, posing as Samir's and Nader's relatives. Nader had thought about what he was going to say for some time. He stopped the music playing in the car and talked to Samir quietly, making sure the woman in the back couldn't hear. He said, "We have so much money in the car. This money won't go to our people. I know where it goes. Protests and demonstrations cost nothing, their lavish lives cost more. Their houses, their everything. They are selling weapons and making money as our people die. They are selling weapons to both sides; it is a weapons business, not a war for a cause. What is the cause anyway? Fighting with your neighbour is not a cause; it is a case of violence."

Samir looked both panicked and relieved. "What are you saying?"

Nader had planned to make a deal with the mother in the backseat, and return to the organization saying that they were robbed by another group which they could not identify. The mother, who was offered a bigger amount of money than the organization's, accepted, and the mission was successfully completed until one of the three, unexpectedly, confessed to the wrong friend. Trust is like fire, it can give warmth, but it can also take lives. In this case, the fire took all three lives in different directions.

Now Camilia was sitting in the front row with Wahab, they were both still very moved by Rahman's story and were, in very low voices, discussing how they could help.

Wahab said, "The best practice of aid is to bring them one by one here to the island and to other countries where they are safe. One by one, story by story. When aid is given in this way, you ensure sustainability. You are building lives, saving families. You ensure integrity and credibility."

Camilia was listening carefully to what Wahab was saying when the dim stage lit up with Nader's smile. My Camilia was shocked to see Nader there. Her grey eyes lit up with hope and happiness. I was happy as well to see my Camilia as joyous as I haven't seen her for years.

"Wahab, it's him! The pearl. Him!"

Wahab wanted to inquire further but was silenced by Nader's first words: "Good evening. Let me tell you that I am in trouble. Long story short, a woman sitting among you dropped something earlier today, and I followed her all the way here to give it back. It is hers and if you can return to someone what's theirs, you sometimes are giving back a part of themselves. Sorry, I am rambling now, but I find this very parallel to refugees too. They lost their homes and lives, and someone has to give it back to them. It is theirs. We all came to this world to live, not to die.

"My name is Nader Madani and I am impersonating the originally scheduled speaker because this is the only way left for me. I did not want to give up and I found my way to be here. I apologize to the organizers of the event.

"As I carry this pearl to return it back to a lady sitting among you, we all have to return back some rights that we, the international community, saw and partook in depriving the refugees of. Now may I ask for this lady to stand up?"

My Camilia never liked public attention. She always turned red when her driver or maid paid her a compliment about a beautiful dress she wore, or a nice hairdo. But as Nader had opened a new gate in her life, she stood up, saying in the loudest voice I had ever heard from her: "Thank you. You are not only someone who returned a pearl, but you brought light to us tonight with inspiration. Thank you. Thank you."

Nader smiled but as the audience clapped, he yelled into the microphone: "Stop. No more clapping and rewarding."

The crowd was astonished by his tone and fell silent. He then went back to his speech. "I have made a mistake, and because I believe mistakes are called experiences in a world of love and forgiveness, I am going to confess."

Nader was going to continue the story, telling the crowd about Lia and her mission when he heard Lia's voice in his ear: "You've already made one stupid move, don't do the second because you will be deported from the island before dawn. You understand?"

Fear won the standoff and silence filled the room for a minute before Nader disappeared backstage.

The last time Nader experienced such a threat was after the organization had grown suspicious about the story he, Samir and their ally, the mother, told. He was questioned constantly by the organization as to where the money actually went.

In truth, the money was spent on different things. First, Samir and Nader supported many families who were in need, mostly refugees in Kabar. Nader and Samir also saved some money to escape the country as soon as Nader graduated school. Samir decided to open a photography studio in Europe. But their plans did not go as desired. A few months later, thanks to threats and force, the organization learned the truth.

Nader had remained close to Rania, the teacher who recruited him initially to the organization. But Samir never liked Rania, who never understood the friendship between him and Nader. One night, Nader told her what he had done with the organization's money and what he, Samir and their ally did on the return from Saghar. Rania had tricked him with false trust, and reported Nader's confession to the organization.

Samir and Nader had a habit of driving in the desert to listen to music and be away from the people and the continuous violence between Saghar and Kabar. The two were very close, and never parted ways. They loved one another, as deeply as brothers do, and despite living in the misery of war, had a planned future to look forward to. That night they went for their usual drive, which would be the last.

Samir sat in the driver's seat, Nader in the passenger's. Music played and the wind blew. Nader had been having a lot of problems with his family; he was in need of attention and affection and found it then with Samir. Nader rested against his shoulder and talked. It was a moment of connection between two souls who found friendship and peace with one another. A car pulled up behind, flashing its hazard lights. A tall man walked out as the two looked in the rear-view mirror.

The tall man, Foad, was an ambitious young man who saw his family suffering from the consequences of the war. His father was ill and could not work. His brother, Riad, was a student and worked part time to afford food for the family. Foad decided to join the same organization Nader was working with, but for a totally different department. His job was to go after people who had betrayed the organization in any way, and to punish them. His wage allowed his family to survive in a country of conflict. Besides the work that paid well, he was a student and wanted to finish his education to leave and start a normal life. Alas, his dream would not come true.

Foad walked to Samir's car and knocked on the window. "Something wrong with my car. I need help."

Nader went back to his seat as Samir opened the window and talked to Foad.

Samir said, "What's going on?"

"Something is wrong with the engine. How are you both doing? Having a good night?"

Samir smiled and said, "It is good to be away from all the military tanks and soldiers. It is just us and nature out here."

Foad then asked for a cigarette, and as Nader was naturally intuitive, he did not really feel comfortable. Still, he got a cigarette out and passed it to him. The three had a conversation about the war, a typical dialogue between the people of Saghar and Kabar. After the cigarettes were put out, Nader remained in the passenger's seat as Samir helped Foad whose car was stopped behind them. Nader could hear a faint conversation and rattling going on outside the car, until there was a moment of silence. And amidst that silence, there was a sudden gunshot. Nader froze in shock, and when he finally gathered the strength to turn around, he witnessed Foad emptying the rest of the bullets into Samir. Samir's body went flying back, an image that would never leave Nader's mind; he then saw Foad approaching the car. Samir had been shot in the chest, and his murderer kept on firing until Samir was absolutely dead.

Samir had always kept a gun in his car after their affiliation with the organization. While shocked at what had just happened and trying to absorb the fact that it was not a dream, Nader pulled the gun from beneath the driver's seat where it was always kept.

The tall man fired a bullet at Nader that went straight into the car, shattering glass but not reaching him. As Foad was changing the cartridge, Nader fired back, getting him in the right side of the neck. Nader found himself firing the remaining bullets with anger and tears, ending the life of Foad who would now be leaving his brother, Riad, and the rest of his family alone. He would also be leaving a troubled life, having been a hit man hired by the organization, something his family did not know about. He did it for his family, for war does not only create troubles, but also the need for survival. His last assignment had just ended the life of a young man, Samir, and started a new chapter for Nader.

Nader ran towards Samir who had already passed away. He saw his loved one full of blood, and his eyes closed on a world of injustice and violence. Nader never understood why he decided to get into the car and drive away, leaving two dead bodies behind and an untold story. It was the first time Nader ever drove in his life, and he couldn't remember anything about the ride back to Kabar—until today.

He drove the car back to Samir's apartment, cleaned it, and not knowing where to go, he made his way to his family's home. His parents were asleep; his siblings as well. He opened the door quietly and ran towards the bed he had slept in as a child. He wished he were a child again, only born in a time where war did not make its way into the lives of people. He could not sleep, so he left for the school where Rania worked, to tell her what happened.

Nader waited for a few hours before Rania arrived at the school, seeming surprised to see him. Of course, she had already been informed, was prepared and knew what to say to Nader. She walked with him as he told her what happened. She pretended not to know Foad or anything about the incident. She cried, hugged Nader and said, "I am so sorry, Nader. I can't believe it. He probably thought you two were a gay couple. I bet he was a homophobic stranger who killed Samir and was going to kill you. You defended yourself, Nader."

Samir's death was filed as a fight—a hate crime—between him and Foad, one murdering the other before committing suicide. The organization did not wish to be exposed, so they paid someone in the government of Kabar to close the file with false facts. At that time, no one but Rania knew the truth: that Nader had killed the intruder, Foad, who was sent by the organization to kill the two "traitors".

Foad's parents were in shock. They were ashamed of what their son had done, at the same time grieving for him. Riad, Foad's young brother, left Kabar immediately as he applied to be a refugee escaping from violence. He wanted to seek a better life, and support his old parents. He had always stayed in Kabar hoping that things got better, but the loss of his brother made him immigrate to the island, where he became an activist in human rights and a film student.

Nader was now under Lia's threat and had to return the pearl, pretending it was the real one. Before the third speaker took the stage, and as the crowd spoke about Nader's personality, Camilia excused herself with Wahab and went backstage to meet Nader and get her pearl back.

Nader was struggling between two thoughts, returning the pearl pretending it was the real one, and lying to my Camilia, or telling her the truth and later dealing with Lia's threat.

Camilia walked into the room he was in, smiling. "My name is Camilia. Thank you, precious young man, for keeping my pearl, it is very important, you can't even imagine."

Nader replied, "Well, you know my name, Nader. Besides the pearl, I am very pleased to meet you. I feel like I want to give you a hug."

So Camilia took Nader in her arms, hugging him like the son she had always wanted. He was smelling her like cats smell their mothers when they're born.

In his earpiece, Lia repeated her threat.

In front of him, he found the warmth he had been seeking. He could not fail it.

His hands reached into his pocket to get the pearl, the fake one Lia had given him. Camilia watched his hand. It wasn't the first time my Camilia encountered deception in her life. Her mission to get her rights and find the identity of my murderer had been met with all sorts of deceit. Some people gave her promises, others fed her lies.

Now it was up to a young man with a very rich history to decide whether my Camilia would be deceived again, or if the truth would be clearly given to her, for once.

This is the case of some human beings living on Earth. They accept reality as it is, not knowing the truth. But the beauty of truth is that it always surfaces with time.

# Chapter Eight: The Situation

The rainstorm had not yet hit the island, and weather reports were indicating that it could very well be delayed until the next morning. But inside the Moroccan Cultural Centre, another storm was about to hit.

Nader was torn by a dilemma: having Lia on the earpiece insisting that he should hand over the fake pearl and get closer to Camilia, and his instinct that told him to be honest.

The silence in the room was broken by Sandra, the event coordinator who came in to speak to Nader. "You tricked me and made your way in. Not a lot of people can say they have done that."

The word *trick* triggered many thoughts for Nader, who at that point made a choice not to trick Camilia and he started talking, looking straight into her eyes. "Camilia, I have something to tell you."

Lia interrupted in Nader's ear: "I hope it is something as we agreed on…."

Nader began to speak his thoughts aloud, which caught Camilia's attention. "No, it is not something we agreed on. Camilia, I don't have your pearl."

Camilia was surprised at what she was hearing and seeing. She did not understand Nader's words, but she found comfort in Nader's big brown eyes, for they were full of stories. He continued. "This morning I had your pearl in my hands. I went around looking for events happening at eight, met with a few people and, in the midst of it all, I lost your pearl."

Camilia smiled at Nader and put her arms around his shoulders. "In the eighty-seven years I have lived, I have never lost anything, but I misplaced almost everything."

"What is the difference?"

"Losing is giving up hope. Misplacing is thinking of the opportunities left to find what you are missing."

"Well, I misplaced your pearl, and I know it is very important. It is either with Riad, Leo, Richard or Amanda. It is not with Lia. I had already lost it when I met her."

Camilia was confused about all the names Nader mentioned, but she continued, "We should then go back to all of these people, and ask them if they have the pearl. I am free the rest of this evening, are you?"

Nader was distracted by Lia who was repeating the same statement in his ear since he admitted that he had lost the pearl: "Do not mention anything about our deal or you will be deported from the island in the morning for interfering with a government assignment." Lia was determined to find out the truth about Camilia. She was dedicated to her career in the investigation unit of the island's police and wanted to excel in her first major assignment. Her job brought her a sense of security and protection, which she felt she had always required in her life. But she was now faced by a young man's decision to either continue with the assignment or cause her problems. As Nader and Camilia started talking, Lia made her way towards them.

The threat Nader heard her repeat did not change his determination to be honest with my Camilia. "Before we make plans to retrace our steps and find the pearl, I have another confession to make."

Timing and luck played in Lia's favour when she interrupted Camilia and Nader. "Here you are, you found her. Congratulations."

My Camilia always had great intuition. She instantly did not feel right about Lia's presence in the room, and said, "Who is this lady?"

Nader did not know what to say, but Lia, being a professional trained to handle this kind of situation, said, "My name is Lia, and I helped Nader get here."

Camilia interrupted. "Well, then, thank you very much. Is there anything else you want from us?"

Lia was not used to my Camilia's straightforward answers. Lia herself was known to be manipulative, and found no alternative but to make up a story, knowing that Nader would not dare to defeat her once again. She said with her usual confidence, "I had a deal with Nader: if he found you, I would take him out for a drink. Would you excuse us for a few minutes before I have to go? I have work very early, and I am afraid I am running late.

I was surprised to see that my Camilia let go of the situation easily and excused herself. "I will be right back for you, Nader; I am going to get my friend Wahab. You two should meet."

Nader did not want Camilia to leave him alone with Lia. "Are you sure? You can stay."

"You finish your business with Lia, and I will be back."

Camilia reminded Nader of another lesson in life: to finish what he had started, and take the consequences, which life translates into experiences. The experience Nader was about to go through was unexpected, with one mistake causing a change in his life and those around him. Lia and Nader were now left in the same room alone, in the backstage area of the Centre.

Lia said, "You were going to tell her everything, are you out of your mind?"

"Why not? She is a very nice lady."

"She is a *mysterious* lady as far as I know. My job is to solve the mystery. You agreed to help me in exchange for staying on the island."

"I changed my mind."

Lia folded her arms. "Fine, change your mind, but don't open your mouth. I can find another way to get to her, but at least appreciate that I led you here, and keep your mouth shut."

"As long as you never hurt her."

"We just want to find out more about her, for the sake of the island's security."

Nader took off the earpiece and gave it back to Lia. "Would you now leave me alone?"

Lia scowled. "Certainly, good luck with your new girlfriend or mother or granny. If you find anything interesting that you want to trade for staying on the island, you know where to find me. Division 13, 5th Avenue." Lia left the room but did not leave Nader alone. He forgot that she had also placed a recorder in one of his pockets. This recorder was about to go on a journey with Nader and Camilia.

Nader was pulling himself together, waiting for Camilia to return with Wahab. He was reminded of the last time he had to pull himself together and gain strength from the universe. It was after that night when he lost Samir and was forced to kill Foad to save his own life. That night, Nader drove back in Samir's car, utterly terrified. He had never driven a car before, but was now behind the wheel running away from the crime scene.

On his way back to the centre of Kabar, he stopped the car on the side of the road and started crying. He did not understand nor did he accept what had just happened. It was a nightmare that he was hoping to wake up from. His upbringing, despite being a refugee, had been very good. His parents were educated and always expected the best of him. He later became a rebel and fought all the time with them; it was around the same time that he joined the organization.

Samir had met Nader when he was looking for a young actor to be featured in a school project. While on a visit to Nader's school for casting, he chose the 13-year-old back then to be acting in his film. The film got Samir a good grade and a friendship that he built with Nader. Nader learned a lot from Samir, who had been living alone for a long time as his family was killed in the war. His life was fairly simple until he met Nader.

The night he died, Samir came to my World, but I did not meet him until later. I assume he met with his family here and looked after Nader for the rest of his time, like I looked after my Camilia. That night too, Nader was left with fear, which is the only self-made dictator we encounter in life. Dictators feed off the control they find in the person they dominate.

When Nader overcame his fear, he had to face reality. He had a feeling that his so-called friend Rania had tricked him, from the very beginning of her recruitment efforts. His assumptions were later proven right. Nader waited a few months until he was able to flee to Ordon, a town neighbouring Kabar from the west side, and a few years later he applied for a scholarship to go study on the island. He ran away and was uncertain about his next step in life until he met my Camilia; things then changed.

My Camilia faced her fears several times in her life. In 1991, by sixty years of age, she had learned a lesson that I want to share with you, the Readers. She learned that fear is not the outcome of a problem, but the cause of a situation. When she feared my family and the people of Saghar, many situations occurred consequently. This defines the concept of fear in our lives. We encounter a situation that we label as a problem, and so it becomes. A situation transforms into a problem when we fear it. Camilia learned this lesson after years of struggle when she was about to give up.

When we are preparing to give up, fear plays a less important role in the situation we find ourselves part of. We reach a point where we have nothing to lose, therefore nothing to fear. Giving up is the enemy of hope, and sometimes it is our best friend because it allows us to let go of fear. We encounter challenges in life, and giving up on something simply means that our energy would now be focused elsewhere. We just have to believe that things took a specific direction for a reason, and let the universe show us the reason as time goes by.

Now back on the island, Camilia was introducing Wahab to Nader.

Wahab said, "So you've lost the pearl?"

"I misplaced it."

Wahab grinned. "That's Camilia's word!"

"I am a good student. So what is the plan now?"

Camilia gave some thought to Nader's question. She found herself talking for the first time to a stranger, Nader, about her personal life. "The missing pearl completes this necklace you see around my neck. This necklace opens a safe in my home where I have kept a secret locked away since 1946, and I have not been sure whether I want it to come out or not. I left it in the locked safe so that after I die, someone might open it and tell what was on my mind. There are people who deserve to know what is in there, but I am scared for others at the same time."

"What's the secret?"

"It is a story that can't be told."

"Why do we need to find the pearl then?"

Camilia said, "We don't need to find the pearl, we need to search for it."

Nader asked, "What is the difference?"

Camilia gestured broadly with her hands. "Finding the pearl is our purpose, searching for it is our journey."

"It was quite a journey to get here...."

Wahab said, "It seems there is another journey awaiting you. Are you doing this tomorrow?"

Camilia shrugged. "It is a beautiful night; the storm is not here until the morning. Why not now? We will go backwards, asking all the people you met and on the way, we can talk."

Nader said, "I know where I can find all of them, except for Leo. I lost him."

Camilia reminded him, "You did not *lose* him, you *misplaced* him, and through our journey, you will find him again if it's meant to be."

Nader said, "How do you know that?"

Camilia said, "An achievement begins with a thought, transforms into a dream, and then we make it our reality."

Nader replied, "That's very wise. But it is almost ten."

Wahab said, "I am not sure if I should join you or not."

"Do you want to?" Camilia asked her friend.

"Yes, but…"

"If it is a 'yes,' there should be no 'but' in your statement."

Wahab grinned. "Fine then, I am joining you and Nader tonight."

They left the Moroccan Cultural Centre, tracing back all the steps that Nader took. They did not know that there were four of them walking, not three. Lia could hear everything that was said through the recorder that streamed live from one of Nader's pockets.

The three, and Lia unknown to them, started by going to the only address Nader knew, Amanda's. He remembered the street name and the old building, number 17. Nader was excited to see Amanda again, and he truly thought that the pearl might be somewhere at her place.

Camilia asked her driver to leave, for she chose to walk around the island with Wahab and Nader, and tell them stories she'd never told anyone before. I wished I were able to speak to my Camilia then, to tell her not to, as Lia was listening, and that one little mistake could lead to bigger problems, for her and everyone involved.

# Chapter Nine: The Reunion

It was getting dark on the island, but three people were about to light the evening with events that would change their lives. Camilia, Wahab and Nader were all night owls, well used to the lack of sleep.

Camilia never slept sometimes because she found the silence of each and every night loud with emotions and memories, mostly of me. The night had always been my favourite time, dead or alive. When I was alive, I thought of the night as the master of the world, taking everyone over through silence and peace. Since I died, the night has been the time when I am the master of my own World of the Dead, living in the heart of the most beautiful woman alive.

Wahab, on the other hand, never slept well because he was not certain as to where life was taking him. Despite his success in business, he was growing older alone, without a wife or a child. He had not learned that it is our choice to feel the way we do about things and events in our lives. For example, while most people choose to grieve when they lose someone, I would recommend celebrating instead. Being dead, I have more freedoms than being alive. I find myself travelling among people I love, in places I always wanted to go to, and I live eternally in the heart of Camilia.

Nader did not sleep much, because he carried pain and guilt with him through life. He considered the sources of these feelings as his biggest problems in life. There were unfair situations he detested, soon to know that they are called experiences that would make him who he would become. He sleepwalked some nights, and spent other nights with insomnia. He always missed Samir, and sometimes found himself feeling guilty for the choices he had made. He also felt fear for the future, as he did not wish to return to Kabar. Samir's murderer, Foad, whom Nader killed, would often appear in the middle of the night, silent but loud in Nader's fearful heart.

So tonight the three were silent, each thinking of what kept them awake in the middle of the night. Nader, who always thought out loud, broke the silence with what was supposed to be something between him and himself: "Why is this pearl so important and worth a night of looking for it?"

Camilia said, "Sixty-six years ago, my husband was killed at our wedding ceremony."

Camilia's statement shocked Nader, who stared at her with his big brown eyes, expecting more. He wasn't the only one who was shocked: I was as well. Camilia was never keen to disclose her past to anyone easily, except the few people who had known her for a long time.

Camilia continued her story with a shattered voice full of dignity, and love for me. "My husband came from a town called Saghar in the Arabian Desert."

Nader said, "I know Saghar, I am from Kabar, right by it."

Camilia, like me, did not believe in a small world of coincidences, but a large space of existence where people meet for a reason. Nader, being from Kabar, brought back to her many memories she had left behind years ago. She smiled and continued. "It is still believed that an extremist group from Kabar killed him."

Nader did not connect Camilia's story to the origin of the war between Saghar and Kabar. History puts dust on the events that initiate wars, and violence erases facts that might be understood to maintain peace. In addition, Camilia was not very convincing and genuine in the way she said her statement.

Nader said, "I am so sorry, I swear it is not anyone I know or I am related to."

"I do not blame you; I lived the journey of my life not to blame. It is a waste of time that we could be using for our own development and growth. Blaming others is the tool of the defeated. Working with others is the road to success."

"Beautifully said. Where is the pearl in all that?"

Again Camilia reminded him, "There is a secret I have carried around with me for sixty-six years now. It is locked in a safe. The twelve pearls, these exact ones and not one less, open this safe. If after my death, the twelve pearls are still there, I have asked for the safe to be opened and for the secret to be out. If the pearl necklace does not make it until then, I have asked for the safe to be burnt."

"What is this secret?"

"You will have to see if the universe is going to let you know that."

Nader did not understand Camilia's last words but Wahab interrupted. "You are from Kabar, how long have you been on the island?"

"A year, almost a year. I am studying here."

Camilia asked, "What are you studying?"

Nader smiled. "A little bit of everything."

Wahab said, "I like that, when I was your age I could do that, now I can't, responsibilities grow with us."

When the three reached Amanda's house, she was sitting at her balcony drinking a glass of wine and smoking. Nader yelled, "Amanda. I am back."

Amanda grinned. "Well I see that, and I also see that you got company. You found her, didn't you?"

"Yes, I did. She is here. Her name is Camilia, and—"

Amanda cut him short. "And what? You came to

apologize and say thank you?"

"Well, that, and I lost the pearl."

"Why am I not surprised?"

"It is not time to be sarcastic. Did I leave it at your place or not?"

Amanda flirted, "Come up and look."

Camilia and Wahab waited for Nader, sitting down on a nearby bench. My Camilia started humming.

Wahab said, "I haven't heard you humming in a long time."

Camilia said, "The pearl, Wahab, I want to see if we will find it or not."

Wahab asked, "What was that secret you were talking about?"

Camilia said, "If I tell you, it would not be a secret anymore!"

Wahab was miffed. "I thought we did not have secrets between us."

Camilia said, "If this pearl is found, the secret will become another told story."

Wahab smirked. "You and mystery: always a unique relationship."

As Wahab and Camilia were talking, Nader came back down, looking disappointed. "The pearl is not up there."

Camilia asked, "Who is next then?"

"I don't know where to find Leo, but I know where Riad and Richard are. Riad is at a gathering happening somewhere close to here. A protest of some kind."

Amanda was listening from her balcony, and joined the conversation. "I know of this protest, I can show you where it is."

Camilia did not like Amanda at first; she felt that the girl was somehow vulgar, having seen her drinking and smoking. But Camilia was judging a book by its cover, a human defect that is common among people in the World of Living. She was not very friendly with Amanda, who soon made her way down and joined Camilia, Wahab and Nader.

Wahab was admiring Amanda's looks; after all, she was a beautiful girl who hid behind a troublemaker's character. Amanda's relationship to her father was similar to the peace process between Saghar and Kabar: she had never found a resolution, yet. She was a rebellious girl since age thirteen, always breaking the rules and finding joy in being the bad girl, just like her father did not wish her to be. Her failed relationships caused anger in her personality, and came across in the choices she made. She dated men and controlled them; she never had a long-term relationship, and always felt under attack from the whole world.

The tension between Amanda and Camilia was obvious, both behaving in a clearly unfriendly way to one another.

Amanda asked, "So why is this pearl very important?"

Camilia huffed, "It is none of your business, young lady."

"I am here to help, and thank you for calling me young. It's a girl's dream come true."

Nader interrupted to ease the tension. "Tell us what you do on the island, Amanda."

"Are you kidding me? We better remain silent here, and get to where we are going."

Amanda was known to get moody when she felt threatened by an attitude or a situation. Now she was facing a woman who was not friendly, nothing new to her, which triggered her defensiveness. The four, and Lia watching and listening to everything, walked down the street, heading towards a crowd that gathered around the Centre.

Camilia and Wahab sat down on a bench, under a streetlight covered by a tree. Amanda was checking out the protest, and Nader went in the crowd looking for Riad. It was a peaceful protest, where everyone lit a candle asking the island's government to assist refugees seeking asylum.

It was a moment that I reflected upon. Nader had killed Riad's brother in self-defence. Riad had looked for the truth all the time, and now the truth was looking for him. I think that this only happens when we really need something, and Riad always wanted to be at peace and know what happened to his brother. He had no clue about his brother's job, nor did he know that the young fellow he had just met, Nader, was the only person who had all the answers.

A protestor on a megaphone said, "Give refugees a

place to call home and another chance in life!"

Nader walked into the crowd, looking at all the faces. He had seen many of the people on the university campus. As he looked for Riad, his pulse increased with the excitement of people calling for rights for people like him, refugees.

There were too many people for him to find Riad, and the excitement was increasing by the second. But this gave him an idea. He went to the leader of the protest, grabbed the megaphone, and ran toward a parked Jeep by the sidewalk. He hopped on its hood with the megaphone in one hand and the flag of Kabar in the other, and said, "Twenty-four years ago I was born a refugee in Kabar, to join 400,000 other refugees, including my grandparents who were displaced because of the war. They lost their homes, their lives, and eventually their rights to dream. The international community promised them, almost seven decades ago, solutions. These promises never saw the light, and people were sunk in darkness.

"Two generations later, the situation has gotten worse. More people, fewer resources, fewer rights, and another war to face. Refugees in Kabar are not allowed to work or attend any public institutions, because Kabar cannot afford to take care of its own people, let alone almost half a million refugees. Where is the international community now?

"I am a refugee here, I am well-educated, and I have things to offer this island. We are not as some media has made us appear to be. We just want to live, we want our rights. We want solutions, we don't want aid spent on unsustainable relief programs. We want a life. We want opportunities. We want to be part of creating a better world, not sitting in darkness waiting for one."

Nader's short speech moved the crowd, even Lia who could see and hear him clearly from where she sat in her car. Camilia and Wahab were moved as well, so was Riad who heard the speech and made his way to the Jeep as Nader descended from its hood.

Nader was jumping off the car when he saw Riad, and all of the sudden ran to him with excitement and a big smile. "I was looking for you."

Riad said, "You made it, did you find the lady and give her the pearl?"

Nader shook his head. "I found the lady, but I lost the pearl. Did I leave it with you?"

Riad shook his head no, but said, "I will help you look for the pearl, it has to be somewhere. This is amazing: you are one stubborn and great man to have found her. But do you know why this pearl is so very important?"

Riad and Nader walked towards Camilia and Wahab, followed by Amanda. Lia, who sat in the car, was listening to what was starting to seem boring to her. Her focus was on getting to know more about Camilia, who so far said nothing and very little about my murder. Lia was intrigued to know what was in the safe and where that safe could be found.

Camilia was captured by Riad's smile and the expression in his eyes. The tall young man caught her attention, as he radiated with positive energy.

Amanda was also captivated by Riad, for a different reason. She found him handsome. She said, "If you don't have the pearl, we need to keep going. Who else are we asking about the pearl Nader?"

Nader said, "There's Leo, who disappeared, and there is Richard."

Wahab said, "We should look for the one who disappeared; he probably has it."

Riad asked, "Is it a very expensive pearl?"

Camilia nodded and replied, "But it also holds a lot of meaning."

Riad wanted to go on with his questions, but Camilia looked uncomfortable, so he dropped it, disappointing Lia who was waiting to hear what the secret was, or any clues about it. The five were now heading towards the bar Richard had mentioned earlier to Nader. They left the crowd that was wrapping up the protest. It had gone well and allowed protestors to send a message for local politicians to respond by granting permits to two hundred refugees seeking asylum.

As they walked, Riad and Amanda talked about the protest. Wahab was starting to feel tired, and had to excuse himself to go back to his hotel. "I am afraid it is time for me to leave you, I have an early morning flight to catch."

Camilia said, "OK dear, thank you for the lovely evening. When do I see you again?"

"I am back on the island next month, I will phone you before leaving tomorrow; I want to know if you found the pearl.'

Camilia gave Wahab a long hug, warm with love. I never liked it when the two were intimate, but luckily it had been only a number of times I could count on one hand.

After he left, Camilia enjoyed the walk with the three young people helping her. She did not know the purpose of their help, but knew that they were embarking on a journey to find the pearl. It was the first time she was mingling with strangers, something she had forgotten how much she enjoyed, excluding Amanda. Camilia and Nader walked in the back, while Riad and Amanda led the way.

To Nader, Camilia whispered, "The pearl is very important to me; I would walk miles to find it. But what is it for you to skip a Saturday night and spend it with an old lady like me?"

Nader said, "I was born to trust the universe, although it gave me little reasons to. I believe that life holds the best for us, but it is up to us to look for it. I had a good feeling when I saw you. I don't really care about the pearl, it is yours and your secret. I care about following what my heart advised me to do, which was to look for you, and be part of this journey."

Camilia listened with full attention, and then a tear

crawled down her face as she replied, "I have led a complicated but beautiful journey. I lived the last sixty-six years thinking about the one man I loved and still do. Secrets are untold stories, and they change reality when they are revealed. I trust the universe too, and if I don't find the pearl, I know that there was a story that was never supposed to be told: my story."

Nader, out of curiosity, asked, "Is it related to your husband's murder?"

Camilia nodded.

I thought I knew everything about my murder, but I could feel that there was something she had kept in that safe that I did *not* know. I always respected Camilia, and if her wish was to hide something from me when alive, then I would not break the rule while dead. Love is unconditional, and shouldn't know anything but respect and loyalty.

Lia, on the other hand, was very curious to know more about my murder, as she believed it would lead to more answers. She observed carefully the four of them as they arrived at the bar. Camilia did not want to walk in, and waited outside with Riad and Amanda. Nader went in and immediately saw his friend Richard, sitting by the bar drinking a glass of beer.

Richard smiled and said, "Hello mate, you're back! Still looking for the lady?"

"No, I found her, but now I am looking for the pearl. Did you find it after I left?"

Richard slapped the bar. "Oh Goodness, you

haven't found the pearl? What's so special about it? Is it made of a rare stone or something?"

Nader looked downtrodden. "No, it's not. Never mind."

Nader was disappointed, said good night, and was making his way out of the bar when Richard yelled, "Last time I saw the pearl was at the restaurant after you finished your meal. You took it out and I did not see you putting it back. Although I called the restaurant, I think you should still go and check there anyway."

Nader found hope and he turned to Richard and said, "Can you take us to the restaurant?"

"It is 1:30 a.m.; they close in half an hour."

"Let's hurry up then."

Nader and Richard left the bar to see Camilia, Amanda and Riad standing in anticipation, rather excited to see Nader walk out with a huge smile.

Camilia asked, "Did you find it with him?"

"No, but Richard saw it last at the restaurant where we ate earlier. He called, but he says it could have fallen somewhere there. It is best that we look."

It was getting very exciting for Lia, as three people whom she was interested in knowing more about, Camilia, Richard and Riad, were all at the same place, and she could hear everything they said.

It was not a long walk to get to the restaurant, and as soon as they arrived, Nader left the group and ran towards Maria, who was smoking a cigarette outside.

"Hello, Maria."

Maria said, "Here comes the big smiley guy again!"

Nader said, "Great you remember me. My friend called about a pearl we lost. Did you ever find it?"

"Well dear, if you lost it here, it's in the garbage now. I cleared your table and cleaned the whole restaurant; it is clean in there, free from even a speck of dust."

Nader asked, "Where do you throw your garbage?"

Maria shook her head. "It doesn't seem to be your night; they just collected the garbage and it's now on its way to the burning spot off the ocean. The boat leaves with sunrise."

"Where is the burning spot?"

Maria said, "All the garbage collected on the island goes on a boat that takes the pile to the middle of the ocean to burn it. They took the garbage already, I am sorry."

"Where is this boat?"

Maria pointed to the port where the boats of the island docked.

Nader said, "Thank you, thank you. Have a great night."

Camilia and the rest knew that Nader had an idea; they could see it on his face as he approached them. He said, "Good news and bad news."

Amanda said, "Start with the bad."

"The pearl is not here."

Camilia sighed. "And the good news?"

"Well, if the pearl was really left on the table or fell anywhere in the restaurant, it would be in the garbage. And the garbage was collected, and is now on that boat that leaves at sunrise to go somewhere in the ocean to be burned."

Riad said, "We need to board that boat then."

Richard added, "I did not expect to end my evening on a garbage boat, but I love the unexpected."

Amanda was not too keen on the idea. She commented, "Looking for a pearl in a huge pile of garbage is ridiculous, and impossible."

Nader objected, "Well it will not be the only ridiculous thing I have done in my life, and nothing is impossible until we give up. So, are you joining us?"

Amanda did not wish to join, but she also did not want to leave Riad and the rest. She was attracted to the Kabar native, and thought it was her opportunity to get to know him. She answered, "I will help you, I have nothing better to do."

Lia was shocked. The five were about to illegally board a boat owned and run by the government of the island. The trip to the burning spot took five hours, and once the boat sailed, Lia would not be able to hear anything: the signal would surely be lost. Lia drove her car down to the port. She wanted to find out the truth about Camilia, Riad, and Richard, and she believed in no limits. I respected that trait in Lia, something I believe more people should do: accept no limits when on a journey to achieve a goal.

The five arrived at the port at 3:00 a.m., after a quick coffee stop at a nearby café. They realized that night owls or not, they needed the caffeine to keep going.

Lia was the first one to board the boat illegally. She was going beyond her duty and forgot about safety and limitations.

Riad went down to the boat alone ahead of the others to find a way to board the group without getting noticed. He was also trying to impress Amanda, whom he was starting to like, thanks to her stunning looks and wry conversation.

Camilia and Nader walked by the ocean, looking at the moon that lit the night. Nader said, "People come together for a reason."

Camilia agreed. "And a purpose. We met because we carry a similar pain, I could see it in your eyes when we met earlier today."

"We have both loved and lost."

Camilia shook her head. "We never lose, we misplace. Remember?"

Nader found himself telling Camilia his story, talking about the organization, his friend Samir, and the dark night when he'd lost him. "I killed a soul that night, in self-defence. I would have been next. I do not carry guilt over this, I had no other choice. I escaped, running away from Kabar to Ordon before, accepting the police report that the two got in a fight, and that one killed the other before committing suicide. Two were dead, and one managed to save his life and escaped with a secret."

Camilia gave Nader a hug and said, "You are safe now. I will be your rock. You are a hero for what you did."

Nader replied, "I am *not* a hero, please don't say that. Heroes are only for fairy tales, an example for us to look up to. We are human beings; we were born with good and evil. *Evil* is a word that is the reverse of *live*. We live, and sometimes we reverse the concept by an evil act."

Camilia insisted, "But what you did was not evil."

Nader replied, "Had I not messed around with the organization and dragged Samir into it, this would have not happened."

Camilia said, "See, what happened is the reason, where you are today is the journey, and where you will be tomorrow is your purpose."

Nader probed, "What is your secret then?"

Camilia smiled. "My secret is that I am challenging the universe to see whether my story should be told or remain buried."

Nader asked, "Do you know who killed your husband?"

"Of course I do."

Camilia took Lia by surprise when she added, "I knew who killed him, and I punished them in the worst possible way."

Nader asked, almost defensively, "Someone from Kabar?"

"No, that was the story told, which was in fact a lie that got the two towns in a war over these many years."

"So the war that I grew up in was based on a lie?"

"Yes my dear, this is what happens in a world that hides secrets: reality becomes what it is believed to be. The people of Saghar and Kabar enhanced their reality with violence, not understanding."

"So, why didn't you say something?"

"Because I too wanted to live."

Nader frowned. "I am confused but I will support anything you do."

Their conversation was interrupted by Riad who, had he arrived earlier, would have heard all that he wanted to know. Instead he said, "I know how we can board this boat. There is a rope in the back; we will climb up that way. Camilia, I will carry you up, don't worry."

The five headed towards the boat where Lia was hiding and listening. It was 4:30 a.m. when the boat sailed with twelve people on board, including the crew. Camilia, Nader, Riad, Amanda and Richard hid in one of the cabins, while Lia sat down on the deck, hiding by the Captain's cabin and listening.

Camilia said, "They will be busy upstairs, no one wants to be around a pile of garbage."

Riad added, "The trip will be about four to five hours, we have plenty of time."

Amanda said, "I will sit down here, watching. In

case anyone comes, I will alert you."

Riad teased, "Good excuse for not picking through a pile of garbage."

Amanda fired back, "Been there, my friend."

Richard was the first to make his way to the pile. He descended into the twelve-foot-deep garbage container without a sound. Before he disappeared, he said, "Camilia, you are not going in. Just wait for us here."

Camilia shook her head. "No, young man with a nice accent, I am going in there in search of my pearl. If you don't look for what you've misplaced, you are not doing your duty in life. One must praise and accept the help of others and join them."

Camilia, Nader, Riad and Richard climbed up the container and dove in. The horrible smell did not matter, only their purpose did. I understood then that aside from Camilia, the rest of them were embarking on this journey because for once, they found a purpose in their life, even though it might not have been entirely clear to them.

An hour into the trip, a noise in the garbage container was heard by one of the crew. He was afraid pirates were aboard. He alerted the rest of the crew, got armed and went down to the first level with two other men. The Captain sent a signal to the port, warning that intruders were on board. I never expected their trip to turn in the way it did, and if one thing I myself learned as an observer of that boat ride, it was that people unite in hardships to face the unknown.

A few minutes after the members of the crew went down to the first level, the storm started again. As lightning and thunder hit, the rough waves caused several cracks in the not so young boat. It was the beginning of a tragic day that sent some of the people on board to the World of the Dead, to *me*.

# Chapter Ten: The Hardships

The storm had finally arrived, with high waves and heavy rain. Each of the people on board was in danger, and each of them felt differently about the situation. The moon was hidden by dark clouds, and water was starting to leak into the hull. The three officers who were checking on the noise were the first to be washed away by the strong flow of water. The Captain and the two crew members on the upper level heard the engine shut down. They lost communication lines to the port, and ran towards the rescue boats. But these small boats altogether could only accommodate a maximum of ten people.

As the Captain released the ropes off one of the boats, a terrified Lia ran up to him and said, "My name is Lia Adams. I am a government official in the Secret Investigation Unit." She showed him her ID that was tucked away in her bra. She always kept it there while on secret missions. She helped the Captain and the two crew members untie the rescue boat ropes, and explained that there were five more people on board.

The Captain looked dumbfounded. "What are you saying?"

"As you heard, there are five other people on board, plus me and your crew."

The Captain said, "Charles, do the math."

Charles, the Captain's assistant, was adding up the numbers as Lia explained. "They boarded your boat because they have lost something and they were looking for it in the garbage."

"And what the hell are *you* doing here?"

"This is not the time. There are only five rescue boats, I see."

The Captain said "Yes, and each boat can take only two people; these things are small."

Charles added, "It means we are leaving two people behind; the waves are getting bigger and we better get out of here. This boat is going to sink."

The Captain said, "Take Lia with you on the first boat." So Lia got in the first rescue boat, and Charles joined her. As she was leaving, she yelled to the Captain: "Please, there is a young man on this boat, Nader. Please rescue him, he has been through a lot of pain, he deserves a better life. And if I do not make it through this storm, make sure he becomes a resident of the island."

The Captain yelled over the roar of the sea, "This is not the time. Now, you two get out of here." The Captain then ordered William, the other crew member left, to go down and get the people to the rescue boats. The boat was sinking for certain as William and the Captain made their way down. The water pushed the three officers, throwing them towards the rescue boats together with Amanda, who was propelled by the same flow.

Camilia, Nader, Richard and Riad were struggling in the container, which was filling with water fast. Riad said, "Camilia, give me your hand."

Camilia said, "No, take Nader first."

Nader resisted. "No, Camilia leave with him and I will manage after."

Camilia said, "Let Richard out now, and take Nader with you."

Riad stood at the edge of the container, giving his hand to Richard as he faced the strong waves. Richard jumped out of the container; he saw the rest of the crew and Amanda getting on the rescue boats. Riad took Nader by the hand, but a strong wave pushed Riad, throwing him into the ocean, out of sight.

And so Riad came to my World, and within the few seconds it took him to get here, he saw all what he had missed in his life, including the truth about his brother's death. In our World, his brother explained to him everything, and they both went to check on their family in Kabar.

Amanda did not see Riad falling, but she felt that a soul she had started to fall in love with was transitioning away from her. All of a sudden, she could see Riad's body drifting away. She yelled, "Riad is in the water. Please save him!"

The Captain, who was helping Amanda and William get away from the sinking boat, replied with a loud and firm voice, "He is gone. We will all be gone if we stay here. Now, go join the rest. You," he pointed to Richard, "get on the boat with Alexander."

Richard noticed his arm was bleeding as he made his way to the rescue boat with Alexander. The last storm he had faced was more metaphorical. It was when he decided to leave the terrorist organization that was forcing him to help them prepare explosives. A few hours before the operation was supposed to be held, Richard confessed to his father about his involvement.

Richard's father quickly arranged for his son to leave Australia, and the group members were all arrested, stopping a tragedy from happening. Richard then moved to the island, starting a new chapter of his life.

Now he was facing life and death again, sharing a rescue boat with Alexander. Another one carried Lia and Charles, the third Amanda and William, and the fourth two crew members. The Captain remained on board, waiting for Nader or Camilia to join him. "He yelled to them, "I know there are two of you there. Please make your way here, I will stay behind."

In the meantime, Nader took Camilia's hand at the lip of the large container and a wave threw both of them down together. Soon my Camilia was freezing, shivering in the cold. I wished I were able to give her warmth, but Nader was doing a good job as he hugged her tight.

Camilia said, "Go with the Captain and leave me behind. It is now time for me to join my husband."

Nader said, "No, please don't say that. You promised to be my rock. And the pearl, we have to find the pearl."

Camilia shook her head. "Looking for the pearl got us here; it is supposed to be an untold story, to bury the pain for me, for him and the two nations that fought for years after his death."

The Captain was starting to loose patience, and had already made his way to the rescue boat, leaving the sinking boat and two people on board, my Camilia and Nader, who yelled, "I will carry Camilia and come join you. Please wait for us."

Camilia said, "Nader, please go. I am an old woman dying anyway. You still have a life ahead of you, and so does the Captain. You have many more stories to tell."

Nader took his jacket and used it to tie his hand to Camilia's; he then moved her hair away from her face and looked deep into her grey eyes. "I won't find the pearl, but I will make sure not to let you go."

Camilia said, "Don't be foolish."

As she uttered her words, she felt something poking her through the jacket tied to her wrist. She slowly put her hand there. It was the missing pearl: it had been in Nader's jacket since he inadvertently picked it up from the restaurant's table. Thus the pearl's purpose was not only to open the safe, but also to lead a group of people into a journey. Camilia took the pearl, looked at it and knew at once it was one of hers; she took the necklace off and gave the twelve pearls to Nader. The Captain couldn't wait as the boat was fully sinking, and he started to sail away on the rescue boat by himself.

Camilia continued talking to Nader, wet and cold, uttering her words with pain. "Go, take this and open the safe. It is in my library behind the painting of a key. You put the twelve pearls in the twelve holes and it will open. Please, do this for me, leave me here and go. It is time for me to join the man I love."

It was a hard decision for Nader to make, but he followed my Camilia's advice as she begged him with her eyes. These were her last words to Nader, right before her first words to me after all these years of absence. Nader left Camilia and did not look behind him; he did not see her take her last breath, because he wanted her alive as a memory forever in his heart, just as Samir was.

As I watched Nader jump into the rescue boat that held the Captain, the storm moved to my world. I saw my surroundings shake, the ground opened up, and here she was again, my Camilia, reunited with me. She came with grace and elegance, stood next to me, put her hand on my shoulder, and her smile lit up those grey eyes that I'd so missed looking into.

She said, "I have missed you."

I replied, "I have watched you almost every day, I heard you speak to me, and always wanted to reply and tell you how much I love you."

"Every day! So you know everything?"

I held her and said, "I only know what I wanted to know and to remember: the beautiful days we spent together and the love we lived. I promised you the day we met that I will never intrude in your life and desires, and I kept my promise. I also promised never to judge you, and I also kept that promise."

Camilia said, "I know who killed you, and the reasons."

"I know too, and now it doesn't matter. In life, we judge. Here, we observe."

Camilia smiled. "And here, I want to live eternally with you."

"We will," I told her. "Now let's look at what is happening where you just came from, I want to see where this pearl is going to take them."

Camilia said, "If Nader doesn't join us here, he is going to open the safe. May I tell you now what is in there?"

"No, I respect your desires, and you wished for the universe to decide on that. It is the same universe you are still in, dead or alive."

As we looked down at the high waves and five rescue boats, the people of the island were watching the news on TV. It was now 7:00 a.m., and the residents woke up to storm alerts and heard that a boat was missing in the ocean.

The storm was still pounding the island, with the rain falling heavily and waves hitting the port aggressively. The destiny of the five rescue boats was unknown.

Adrift at sea, Lia was cold and reflecting upon what had just happened. She was talking to herself: "She is dead, and I may join her soon. All the work I did to prove that I am strong and smart—what a waste of a life, ending in the ocean. If I make it, I am going back to law school. I won't let the circumstances in my life define who I am; I will create myself as I wish. Why did I change into another person? I should have been the captain of my own life, not affected by the waves I came across."

She looked up at the sky and, for the first time in years, she prayed: "God, please let me reach the shore and give me a second chance. "

Amanda, too, looked at the waves surrounding her. She was violently seasick, and also thinking about her life. It is funny how we only get to think seriously about our life when we are about to lose it. I remember that in the last second before that bullet ended my life, I thought about all the bad and good I had done. I was curious to know what Camilia thought about, so I asked and she responded, "I thought only about one thing: You were worth every sacrifice I made, every day I lived, and every purpose I worked for. My life was yours, I proudly ended it with satisfaction, and my journey led me to the destination I love: you."

I replied, "You are my love. You are my hero."

She answered with a smile, referring back to Nader's statement earlier, "Don't call me a hero; they only belong to fairy tales. I did my share of bad deeds that I consider now as experiences, steps that made me reach you."

"What bad deeds are you talking about?"

She answered, surprised, "Didn't you watch me day by day, month by month?"

I replied, "For one year after my death and few months here and there, I distanced myself from you. I chose not to see you in pain, because I could have done nothing from here and it hurt too much."

She gracefully answered, putting her finger on my mouth to keep me silent. "Well, then you missed out on the most important parts of my life. Now let us look at them; I am worried about Nader. It is too early for him to join us here; he needs more time to transform the world, because his story is meant to be told, by him, not by others."

I was confused by this, but I decided to look back at the world you Readers are in.

Amanda was thinking about the time she wasted in a spiral that only brought more negativity to her life. She'd had dreams that the negative cycle took her away from. She'd had love that she kept to herself, fearing to share in the event that her situation with her father would repeat itself. However, like the fights between Kabar and Saghar were based on false assumptions, so were Amanda's fears. She chose to be rebellious because her father chose to be overprotective. Now all she thought about was him. She was allowing herself to think about the positive things her father brought to her life: the first time he taught her how to ride a bike, the gifts he put under the Christmas tree that he took nights to decorate, the time he drove her to swimming classes in the morning, his constant affection despite her own attitude, and much more. She had a smile on her face and looked at the sky, like Lia did, and said, "Father, I hope I make it today and see you to tell you how much I love you, because I never did so in my life. I knew you sacrificed a lot for me, but I always wanted more, because I felt that the world was not enough for me. I had two roads to take, a negative one of conflict, or a positive one of being creative. I took the wrong path, it seems."

Then Amanda, who had never prayed in her life, looked at the sky and said: "God, please allow me to make it. I need to try the other path in life, the right path that I have missed."

I wanted to tell Amanda that she had not missed anything yet, and that soon enough she would be one of the survivors and take the positive route of living.

Camilia thought about Wahab, and looked at the side of the island, where he was drinking his coffee in the hotel's lobby and watching the news. On television, a reporter said, "A storm has hit the island. Flights are cancelled. A boat has been lost in the ocean with six crew members. They are missing, along with a few people who were reported by the Captain to be illegally on board shortly before the boat sank."

Wahab mused aloud, "Flight's cancelled, another day on the island. I should call Camilia and go see what happened with her and the pearl thing. She's probably still asleep." Wahab then tried to call Camilia, and got no answer.

From here, she looked at him and explained to me, "He is a very special man, a dear friend who helped me through all the storms of life."

I said, with a little bit of jealousy, of course, "You spent more time with him than you did with me."

She immediately responded, "That's not true, you know better than that. I never left you. I was always yours, and only yours."

Her words made me smile as I looked down at Richard, who was on the boat with Alexander. He asked, "Do you think we will make it?"

Alexander said, "If they find us we will, and if the waves do not push us somewhere deeper in the ocean. As long as the waves don't hit the island, I am fine. I have two kids and they are probably on their way to school now, terrified."

"Boys?"

"Yes, two young boys. My two princes, and my

princess. She is my high school sweetheart, my wife." Meanwhile, his high school sweetheart, Anna, was watching the news from home. She was distraught, praying for his return. Anna was a strong believer in thoughts creating reality, and she focused on the positive. She knew and felt that in a few hours, Alexander would be one of the survivors who would reach the shore. However, sometimes having a thought becomes weaker than the universe's desire to create a new experience for us. As she clenched her hands and watched the news, a huge wave took away Alexander and Richard, who joined our world a few seconds after the water washed away their bodies, throwing them deep in the ocean.

Alexander's last thought was of the happiest time of his life, a few seconds before he left to go to work that morning. He had made love to his wife, showered, watched her smile, kissed his two boys on their foreheads as they slept, and left before dawn. He did not know then that he would not return.

Richard's last thought was also a positive one, as he thought about all the places that he had travelled to earlier in his life. He thought about the choices he'd made, now being a strong believer that it all happened for one reason: for him to see as much of the world as he could, because somewhere in his conscious, he knew that he was not staying for much longer in the world you, the Readers, live in.

So Richard and Alexander joined us, but we never

saw them. Richard went right away to a spot where he could see all his loved ones, and Alexander watched his boys and wife for the rest of their life, narrating his story like I have been doing for Camilia.

Now there were four boats floating. Nader and the Captain were on the same one, along with the pearl necklace.

The Captain said, "What were you doing aboard my boat?"

Nader sighed. "Long story."

The Captain said, "Well, do you want to share it, since we might be dying soon?"

Nader managed to laugh. "Some stories are meant not to be told—my dear Camilia told me this just a few minutes ago before she left this earth. If we make it to the shore, I will tell you my story."

The Captain scoffed. "Juvenile behaviour, from start to finish. You were not supposed to be on board, and you are too young to die. Unlike me: I am an old lonely man who sails boats."

"You are not married?"

"No, I always wanted to have fun, and was scared of stability. I was selfish. I always said 'tomorrow, tomorrow'; and here is tomorrow: dying on a boat."

"Don't say that, I have a feeling we will make it."

The Captain said, "You will, I will not." The Captain was being hard on himself, fearing the criticism that the residents of the island would direct at him. Only negative thoughts came to his mind, and statements he would be hearing, like "Why did you sail if you knew there was a storm coming?" and "You have always been a selfish person, not surprising, Captain." And as these statements of false fear raced in his mind, he jumped off the boat into the ocean, ending his life and leaving Nader alone on the rescue boat.

The Captain's last thoughts were negative, and it showed in the journey he led after his death. He sat in a valley far away from the island, as lonely as when he was living. Through his loneliness, he looked at people and lived through their lives, being observant at all times. These were the choices he had made; this was the destination he had sought.

Now Nader was alone, in silence. He could not see the other rescue boats because of the high waves, but he was a firm believer that he would make it through, until his confidence was shaken by a huge wave that hit his boat, breaking it in two pieces and throwing him miles away from the shore.

As his small boat broke apart, so did Camilia's heart, I could feel it. I had to comfort her, with words of hope. "He at least will join us here; it is not a bad place, dear. I have been living here for sixty-six years, and it can be at times better than living there."

As the waves took Nader miles away, the storm hit harder. Lia's boat was pushed in the right direction by a huge wave. She and Charles were rescued by a medical team, and as they dried her, she reported what had happened, telling about Nader, Camilia and the rest, without getting into the details of the story.

Wahab was on the phone with the airline when he heard the news: "Lia Adams and Charles Anderson are two survivors of the sinking boat. Lia Adams is a police agent who was not supposed to be on the boat, but was on public service mission investigating a group of five people."

Meanwhile, Leo was waking to his mother telling him to check the news. Shortly after he heard the news reporter mentioning Nader's name, he ran down to the port. It was the first time he ever disobeyed his mother, who insisted that he must stay home to help with chores.

He had dreamt about Nader the night before, but could not remember the dream. I can tell him that he dreamt what was about to happen. He had not left Nader the day before, as Nader assumed. He had gone to speak with his mother on the phone, who demanded that he came back home, but later realized that he had to fulfil his promise. He stopped at the island's information centre to ask about the event, and when he returned to the cafe, late as he always was, he could not find Nader, who had already left.

There was a spark of admiration between the two, a strong connection that they had developed in a short span of time. Now Leo was worried that Nader thought of him as a person who defeated him, but Nader had not stopped thinking about Leo, even when he closed his eyes the second before the wave threw him in the ocean.

Leo prayed for Nader, so did Camilia, and shortly after, myself. Being more than an observer and engaging with more feelings, I felt for the young man who had seen many challenges, and truly did deserve a better life. However, sometimes it is one chance that we are meant to experience, not another one. If we have lived our life in pain, that pain may one day become an example of survival for others—which Nader's story would soon be.

The other two boats with Amanda and the crew members who survived joined Lia on shore a few minutes after. They were all welcomed by a medical crew and taken into government care, each after briefing the media about what happened. Amanda refused to talk to anyone, and made her way to call her father as soon as she was done with her medical check up. She would live with her parents again for the next year before she met a man she would love and marry.

The officers did not understand what was happening, because they never had the chance to talk to anyone about what the "pearl crew," as I will call it now, was doing on the boat. It was left up to Lia to handle the media. She gave a statement: "There were twelve people aboard the boat I was on. Six crew members, only four of whom have made it here thus far. Still missing are the Captain and Alexander Gardiner. There were also six people, myself included, who were not supposed to be on the boat, but adventure and courage took them away. Besides me, Amanda Donaldson is the only survivor up to now. I can confirm the passing of Camilia Vidal, a European lady who lived on the island, and of Riad Rahal. Nader Madani, a young hero, in the true sense of the word, remains missing."

Leo was devastated by the news, but felt that Nader was still alive. He could recall those big brown eyes, and he could feel Nader calling for him. Meanwhile, Wahab went to the bar of the hotel, ordered Camilia's favourite champagne and opened it to salute her. She, watching, appreciated what he was doing as it was something each promised the other to do if he or she died first.

On the other side of the island, where the forest was and many miles away from the port, a new chapter was just starting. A huge wave threw Nader, who still clutched the pearl necklace that he'd tied to his wrist. He landed on the shore with a broken arm, as he noticed seconds after he took his first few breaths on land, expelling water and finding it hard to breathe. He'd seen a glimpse of our World of the Dead as he struggled there in the ocean; he'd seen Samir's face telling him it was too early, and Camilia saying the same. Finally, with persistence, he reached the shore. He then opened his eyes, feeling dizzy and in much pain. He saw the necklace tied around his wrist and arm, and sighed with relief.

The second that Nader breathed again the storm stopped, leaving a wrecked seaside and an abandoned Nader seeking help. And of course, it also left many stories to finally be told.

# Chapter Eleven: The Confessions
*Part One*

After every night, there is a morning. I have always disagreed with people who think of the night as a dark space of existence: haven't they thought about the light of the moon and the millions of stars? There is a night, and there is a morning.

For all the years I lived, I learned that life is all about perception. We perceive things in a certain way, and it becomes the reality we live. We should enjoy the night, so that we have better mornings. Why wake up in a state of darkness when we can choose to always be in the light?

My name is Camilia Vidal, and I died a few hours ago aboard a sinking boat by the island I lived on for my last ten years. I was looking for a pearl that opens a safe where I kept a secret, but the universe chose to keep that pearl in the hands of Nader, a young man who might still make it and reveal what I kept to myself for years.

I will confess now that earlier today when Nader

helped me and my necklace broke, I dropped the pearl on purpose. I wanted my kept secret to be told by the universe, if it was meant to be. Life is too short to wait for an experience to happen, sometimes you must create it.

My husband, who has been narrating my story to you from what I understand, has told the events from his perspective. The lens by which he saw the reality stems deep from his heart, where all that was left there was his love for me, the woman who truly loved him, although I wasn't supposed to.

Now he is here again, next to me, giving me the sense of security and love that I always found with him. It is a gift that he gave me, and I gave him many gifts in return.

With me as well is Nader, not physically, but a memory and a living journey I will observe for however many years he lasts in that world. As he finally breathed again, he was thinking about me. He found himself on the shores of the island, right by the deserted forest, alone, cold and hungry.

It was nine o'clock that morning when the storm stopped, after causing major damages to the pretty island. Lia, the woman whom at first I did not like gave her version in a full statement to the local authorities. She kept to herself what Nader told me about his self-defence crime, and of course, she never had the time to know my full story—and will not, unless that safe opens.

Leo, the young man who Nader misplaced on the island, meanwhile made his way to the emergency centre, set to search for the missing people, unaware that Nader had survived and was on land, a few miles away. He went to Lia, who was leading the group with a few other men:

"I want to help, who is missing?"

"The Captain, a crew member, Richard and Nader."

"What can I do?"

"I don't know yet, the search will begin on the island and in the water in an hour. We are waiting for the storm to completely calm down."

Leo yelled, "An hour! That is way too long; what if they are injured?" Leo was known for his immediate reactions that were fuelled by passion, and which made him seem aggressive to some people. An officer on the rescue team interfered: "We are doing our best to make sure they are found. There is nothing you can do but wait."

Leo, like me most of the time, never knew how to give up. He made his way back to his car, kicking the stones that were piled up by the shore. The young people of the island were known to be active in social media, which sparked an idea for Leo. On Twitter, he posted a message that a young man named Nader was missing. His message read: "A dear friend, and three other people, went missing after their boat sunk during last night's storm. Let's get on it and save their lives. #FindNader"

Within seconds, hundreds of young people had read the message and left their homes to head toward the shore and look for the four missing people. While traditional media is produced and broadcasted by huge corporations, social media is run by the public. People feel safer and closer to each other after all the hardships humanity has seen. Traditional media always moved the masses, with time and enough manipulation. Social media changes the masses, with information straight from the people with their own words and passions.

Leo engaged the residents of the island, as the local authorities asked people to remain calm. They feared losing more lives, especially when they did not know yet if the storm was to come back.

Khaled was an illegal immigrant on the island; he had been hiding from the authorities for years now. He arrived from another island a few years earlier—funny that I had run into him only once, when I walked by the shores of the island, some years ago.

He spent all his time in a hut he built in the forest, and worked under-the-table jobs, cutting down trees and selling firewood. He made a decent living for him and his dog. Like all the rest of the island's young residents, he had an internet connection and was active on social media. He just woke up after sleeping through the storm. He saw the media coverage of the aftermath, and he also read Leo's Tweet, but was too lazy to do anything about it.

Khaled had lost the excitement he used to have about life, because he was mired in fear, like our boat was mired in the ocean. He grabbed his cup of coffee and sat outside smoking his cigarette, a habit he had always wanted to quit. As he lit his first cigarette, he wondered about what would be next in his life, and as the thought travelled through his mind, he saw something moving on the shore nearby.

He threw his cigarette away, swearing that it would be his last one, and ran towards the shore where he saw Nader, bruised, bleeding and calling for help. He had been there for hours and was in need of immediate medical care. Nader uttered, blood coming from his lips, "Take this, it is a pearl necklace."

Khaled was amazed. "I don't need a necklace, we need to get help. Are you one of the people who were on the boat?"

"Yes, I am Nader."

Khaled said, "Stay here, and don't move." He ran to his hut to get a blanket and his phone to call an ambulance. He went back, waiting for the ambulance to arrive. He did not wish to move Nader, as he knew that he could do more harm than good; instead he gave him water. It was a few minutes before the helicopter arrived at the location Khaled had mentioned.

For the first time in years, Khaled spoke to the authorities and overcame his fear. He was always scared that he would be deported to the island he came from, where a war between the residents and the pirates waged continuously. I never understood why the world had such barriers, forcing us to exist in places we were not supposed to live. Freedom is the basic right for happiness that only some practice. My happiness was found on the island in 2002, and when I arrived, with all the mental luggage I carried, I found peace, so I settled in. Happiness is not a hard equation, it is only about us trusting our instincts to discover the unknowns, and the result will always be the same: just as we desired it.

Khaled found a purpose that morning: to help an injured victim of a disaster that happened near him. In the few minutes before the ambulance helicopter arrived, Khaled thought about life and how it can end in a blink of an eye.

As the medical team took Nader and flew him away, Khaled thought about the unknowns of his life. What happened that morning was a sign from the universe that he needed to go through the process of refugee claim on the island, and face his fears instead of sinking in them.

So Khaled that morning wrote on Twitter an update that Nader was found and on his way to the island's hospital. His Tweet would be shared by many residents of the island, and he would become one of their news reporters a few years down the road, all from a single instance that he allowed to change his life.

Leo and my best friend Wahab knew that Nader

was found alive, thanks to social media. Nader told the medical team that the Captain died, choosing not to disclose that he'd committed suicide, for reasons I discovered later. He made the Captain a hero, something Nader did not want to be called. Now, I understand that a hero is a title people deserve at the end of their life journey, just as a means to carry the name into the future. It is like the son we leave behind, the achievements that have our names and the people that we built relationships with. Richard and Alexander were still missing, and they would not be found for a month, forcing their families into hope, which eventually turned to disappointment. Hope is the belief of two possibilities, and sometimes it is beyond the control of people to know which possibility destiny takes, and which story it adds to our life.

Nader arrived at the island hospital at the same time as Lia, Leo, Wahab and Amanda. Doctors checked him. He had a broken wrist but I was there by soul, holding his hand, and the brave fellow felt it. He kept checking on my pearl necklace every now and then, keeping it safe like I now want it to be, to open the safe and let the world know what I kept hidden.

I was born in Paris in 1925, to a mother and father who were strict, religious and very harsh on me. I always thought of the world as bigger than it actually was, and did not want my freedom to be oppressed by the strictness of my parents. I left home when I was fourteen, to a convent that my mother found fit for me, run by even stricter people. I was a very quiet and polite girl. The nuns were not always nice to us, but I knew that I had to be nice in order to get good treatment.

I left the school when I was seventeen, heading to my first year of college, studying languages. In my first year of studies, I had a friend who was getting his Master's. We met at the café on campus, and he liked me instantly. I did not like him very much at first sight, but later he became like the brother I never had.

For the first few months, we would go together to many places, discovering Paris, writing poetry, drawing and studying. People assumed we were in love, while in fact we were like siblings. After a few months into university, I ran short of money. Paul knew, and for the first time he admitted he'd lied to me: "I lied to you Camilia, my parents are not rich as I said, and they don't pay for anything I have."

I asked what he lived off then, and he continued, telling me the truth. "I am a secret agent for a private corporation; working with countries we colonized to put our hands on their resources. We need to expand as a country and an empire after the war."

I was not shocked but intrigued to know more, and Paul said, "I have a job for you, I have already talked to my supervisors, and you are what they are looking for."

I fearfully inquired more, and he explained further

as I sipped a glass of wine, thinking of the adventure I was about to take. "There are two towns, Saghar and Kabar in the Arabian Desert. They are two united towns that have many armed men who are against our country's colonial power. We want the two towns to fight, we want them to be in conflict, so that our corporations can intervene and take control over the resources. We have lost a lot in the World War, and we need to think of our future. You will have one of the main roles for this mission, for your country."

I always trusted Paul and never doubted for a second that he only wanted the best for me. I also loved my country, and was ready to do anything for it. So for the next few months, I got the necessary training, and was then ready to pose as a translator for the private corporation. I was asked to visit Saghar and meet the man who later became my husband. The mission was clear to me from the beginning: I get him to fall in love with me, for he was a womanizer according to the reports, and to marry me so that his production plants became mine.

My husband's murder would be blamed on Kabar, who did not like from the beginning that he married a foreigner, of a different religion and culture. The blame would lead to war, and so it did. The war helped the private corporation I worked for to take control over the oil plants in Kabar, and the water in Saghar. My legal fight to gain the production plants was staged for the authenticity of the mission. The organizers knew that a small conflict was only meant to become bigger, and hatred was easy to spread. My demands, and my husband's family, fuelled the war and gave that private corporation a valid excuse to always be present in the region.

I knew about the murder of my husband from the first day I met him. I fell in love with him, truly and outside of the mission I'd been sent on, what I knew became what I suffered from. On one hand, I was for the first time in my life falling in love with a great man; on the other hand, I was on an assignment and had been told from the beginning that there was no turning back.

Only a few days before my wedding, which was planned to be my husband's murder, I demanded a meeting with Paul and my supervisor back in France. They both flew and met me in Saghar. My husband, whom I loved dearly with all my heart, knew Paul and Samuel, as I had introduced them to him a few months before. The three of us went on a long walk in the desert, and I asked if the plan could change.

Samuel said, "Paul has been asking for a change of the plan, but no, your husband-to-be is one of the wealthiest people of Saghar, and there is already tension from Kabar residents about his wedding."

Paul commented, "I know it must be very hard."

Samuel continued, "With our work, there is nothing hard or easy, there is only one way that things are supposed to be."

I suggested, "But can they just injure him, do they really have to kill him?"

Samuel asked, "Are you in love with him?"

I said, "It is not about that."

"What is it about then?" Samuel's aggressive approach to me was the end of that conversation. My questions and request brought anger to him and the higher people he worked for.

After my husband's death, I left Saghar for France, and then I went to Italy where I escaped the world for a whole year, and sank in my own misery and pain.

The mission achieved its purpose. As soon as the war started, the private corporation I worked for entered Saghar and Kabar, buying resources and companies from residents for cheap. They feared that they were going to lose it in the war, anyway. I only got some money for doing my job. I had to pretend that I was trying to find out who killed my husband, sitting down with lawyers for fifty-six years after his murder, being a puppet for the bigger private corporation. I understand why Lia was trying to investigate me: I ran away from Europe after the case was closed, taking with me enough money to live on comfortably, and a memory that never died, even after I did. Many people in Europe thought I'd died, as I never continued the search for the identity of my husband's murderers, who were my employers. My assignment and role eventually came to an end, and I was drowning in guilt.

To my husband, standing silently by my side, I said, "Forgive me."

My husband said, "For what?"

"For what I just confessed."

"I've known since I came here who killed me. Abu Khalil, a friend of mine, told me everything. You see, they did not kill my love. I respected you and did not wish to know more about your past or private life because love knows no judgment, so what's the difference in remembering what hurts? I only chose to see the good in you, Camilia, I did not want to look at what you thought of as bad. Things happen for a reason, and my death changed the lives of many."

I wept. "I am sorry for the people of Saghar and Kabar, and the war that went on between the two nations is the only guilt I carried in my life. For you, I only carried love. I could not stop what the mission was, because we were both going to get killed then, Samuel was clear about this."

"You did what you had to do. Is this what you wrote and hid in the safe?"

"In the safe, I left my journal, your picture and a secret."

"*Another* secret?"

"The secret is the most important part, for it is what I did for you."

"Why don't you tell me now?"

"Let's look down at Nader now. Remember that this is not up to me, it is up to him and to where the journey will lead him."

So my husband went into silence as we both looked at the hospital where Leo sat by Nader's bed, as Lia and Wahab waited outside the room.

Leo's upbringing had been controlled by fears created by his mother and father, who were authoritative and always expected the best from him. Living in fear, that became his only perspective. He never invested time in his other feelings, like love and admiration for things around him in life. Since he met Nader, though, his heart turned from a dry seed into a growing plant full of living energy. He was now focusing on giving him love and care.

Outside the room, Lia told Wahab all that happened, which brought my best friend to tears, remembering all the memories we'd created together. She said, "And Nader did not leave her until she died, she asked him to leave her behind on the boat, dying in peace."

Wahab asked, "And did the pearls make it to shore?"

"They did, the twelve of them are with Nader, and I think it is up to him to open the safe or not, for he saved them with his life."

"Will you help him stay on the island?"

Lia nodded. "He is one of us now, and I will do my best to make sure he has access to a better life. We would be proud to have him here."

Wahab and Lia's conversation ended as Leo joined

them, and he had heard all that Lia said. Humanity comes together during celebrations and hardship, and gets separated during times of selfish thoughts that are the tools by which nations express themselves. All nations celebrate and grieve, for these are human feelings that, if we concentrate on them rather than on conflict and the differences between us, we would ensure world peace.

Saghar and Kabar forgot about what brought the two nations together; they only focused on the conflict that was based on false and manipulated assumptions. I was a war child because I helped to start one. Nader was a war child because he was used by people who worked backstage in a context of violence. Amanda and Lia also were war children. War is not only performed by weapons, it is the chaos that our societies enter into, a negative spiral that claims the life of many. Who is to be blamed? Nobody. Who is to work for a better world? Everybody.

*Part Two*

My Camilia found me in silence for some time after her confession. It hurt me to see her in pain saying something I knew but purposefully chose not to remember. Love does not know circumstances or conditions; it only knows existence and influence. I broke the silence as she went back into it, observing the island and whom at this stage she considered as a son, Nader.

For the next few days after that morning, Camilia and I went to the places we always wanted to go to. We started our journey in Bethlehem where Jesus was born. We saw people fighting, but it would only be a few more years before the people in conflict revolted against their governments and made the choice to live in peace.

We then went to the valley that separates Syria and Turkey, where we also saw violence, but we did not focus on it. We knew that in a few years, the people of these countries would fight a third World War, and after a new phase of colonization in modern terms, the countries would go back to rebuilding their nations, learning that war destroys dreams and generations. We enjoyed looking at the ancient ruins, and as we sat on a cliff, I asked Camilia, "Where do you want to go now?"

Camilia took my hand and said, "Love does not know judgment, you taught me that."

I nodded my head in agreement, not knowing what she would say next.

"When I was living, there were so many things I wanted to do. I couldn't. I simply couldn't because of all the rules and laws."

I asked her what these things were.

"There are many people who are unhappy because of poverty, while others have more than enough, not appreciating, like you, when you were alive."

I replied "Are you judging now?"

She continued, "No, I am trying to explain what I wish to do. I want to go to Saghar. I miss the town, the people. I only see them in the news, part of war stories that break my heart."

I did not wish to do anything but what she wanted, and within seconds we were at the well of Saghar. The town had changed, and war had wiped off its sparkle. I have come here every few years to check on whoever remains from my family. Some I met, others I avoided. Camilia looked at Saghar with sadness and fear.

We went to one home and saw two brothers, who were sleeping with smiles on their face. They had eaten their dinner, they were excited for school the next morning, and this defined their contentment. There were no tears to dry. In a second home we saw a young girl who slept with her teddy bear; she dreamt of fairy tales and laughed as she slept. Hamza, the boy we went to last, and who was earlier crying from the bombs that were exploding around Saghar, slept with a smile as he dreamt of his favourite cartoon character taking him on a journey around his animated world away from war. These children defined happiness by the simplest things, and when they were awakened by the night, it was the action of adults that brought them tears and misery.

As we went around Saghar, I could feel Camilia's fear and guilt as well. I could not explain her feelings, but when I was about to ask her, she interrupted. It was time to return to the island now, as Camilia felt something she had feared for years. She looked at me, with the deep grey eyes that I admired, and said, "When we leave it up to the universe to define our destiny, we have to accept what the universe determines as the best for us. Nader has the pearls, and I feel he is close to the safe now; it is time to return to the island. I want to be there with you when the safe opens."

Within minutes, we were back at the island sitting down on a rock by the shore, close to the port. I was anxious for this safe to open, and was hoping that Nader would not lose a pearl or two. On the rock by us, we saw a few people from the World of the Dead sitting down. Riad and Samir were there, and a conversation started between the two.

Riad asked, "Who are you?"

"My name is Samir, a very good friend of Nader's, and the person your brother killed."

Riad said, "When I died, my brother told me everything. He only wanted a job to support us, his family. He chose the wrong path and that organization used him."

"Don't explain, I have forgiven him."

"Like I have forgiven Nader for taking my brother away from us, as unfortunately he had no other choice. He broke my mother's heart and I lived my last few years trying to find out who killed him."

Samir said, "In this world, forgiveness is easy. I noticed that we only carry love with us, nothing else. Even the saddest memories we lived become an experience we look at now with pride, because of the journey we lived. Look at him, I see myself through him."

"Nader?"

"Yes, through love, I can be alive while dead, forever."

Riad agreed. "Love doesn't know a state of existence, a requirement or condition of being or living. It only knows how to be eternal."

"Who is she?" Samir was asking about my Camilia, who overheard what he said.

"My name is Camilia, and I too was part of Nader's journey, in my last day. He told me about you. I am glad I found you."

Samir said, "You have beautiful eyes, they hold many stories you probably brought from the other life."

Camilia smiled at him. "I have many, but only one matters. I have a feeling you will know about it soon."

We all watched as Nader walked down the street with Lia, Wahab and Leo, heading towards my Camilia's home. Lia had obtained a permit to enter so that Nader could get the safe. The four of us here looked, soon joined by many of the people who loved me or whom I have loved.

We were all looking at the huge home of Camilia, who was very pleased that the pearls found their way through all this journey, and that a secret she'd kept was about to be revealed.

Nader walked into her home, leaving the other three outside, as he wished to be alone, just like my Camilia asked him. He looked around the tidy and clean home, decorated with souvenirs from all over the world. He walked in the rooms until my Camilia's spirit guided him towards the library where the safe was kept. The young man was shivering, and so was my Camilia. Soon enough, Nader would be reading her story, her job, her mission, my murder and all that her journal contained; up to the date she locked the safe. She loved me, dearly and warmly. She was loyal to me and although on a mission, she put her life in danger for honest feelings she developed as she spent every second with me. She fell in love with me at first sight, and so she challenged her job and role.

I knew most of what the journal said about Camilia's role in my murder. Since my death, I never focused on anything but the good in Camilia; it was my choice, and I hold it with no regrets. But there was one thing, among a few other things I did not know, which brought me shock and confirmation that I indeed, had fallen in love with the most beautiful soul there is.

What Nader knew at this point was capable of changing the realities of Saghar and Kabar. The key for the peace between the two countries was in his hands, the secret revealing that it was not the people of Kabar who killed me, but a foreign power that wished to take control and found in this conflict the answer to their interests. It was a fabricated event, meant to insert danger and harm between the towns. When a nation goes into conflict, it gives up many of its rights and resources.

The last paragraph that my Camilia added to her journal, before she locked the safe, is now capable of changing the destiny of one man as well, who, like Camilia, has many rights to claim. I never had the chance to look at what Camilia wrote that day, I missed what could have changed my journey after death as well. It all happens for a reason, and now a man can have all the reasons to cause change.

Her last paragraph read:

"The night before your murder, and witnessed by the moon of the desert, I gave up my virginity to you because I knew I would not have the chance to do so after we married. You made love to me, and I made sure to carry your legacy for nine months after. I will escape now to save our child and give him away, so that no one touches him with harm, and he or she grows up with love and power. If this safe ever opens, our child needs to know, needs to claim his rights. If this safe never opens, it means that our child lives forever after in peace, without carrying pain and revenge. I don't want people to hurt him knowing that he is my son, the son of a traitor. I am full of regrets, but I shall live to keep my son safe for now, with the memory of your love eternally in my heart."

So Camilia bore a child, a boy who she gave up for adoption so that her work would not harm him, nor would the people of Kabar and Saghar. As Nader walked outside Camilia's house where Wahab, Lia and Leo ran towards him to know what the secret was, I looked at the deep grey eyes of my Camilia and said, "Thank you. Deep inside me, I knew there were two pieces of me left in that world. Now, there is one here with me, one is there and a third joined. I will live through Nader's journey to find our son so that he knows the truth and unites my people with those of Kabar. War ends when some stories are told the way they are, and peace is celebrated when stories are told with clarity, forgiveness, love and acceptance. Creativity and success will always leak through the cracks of broken hearts."

# Index of characters

The Narrator
Abu Khalil: Bookstore owner in Kabar
Alexander GARDINER: Boat crew
Ali SALAM: Richard's friend
Amanda DONALDSON: Student
Ayham SOLTAN: Narrator's eldest brother
Camilia VIDAL: Narrator's wife
Charles ANDERSON: Boat crew
Dalida BATTISTA: Landlord
Eric BERTRAND: Narrator's French friend
Foad R.: Kabar resident
Frédéric BOURGET: Camilia's lawyer
Ghassan SOLTAN: Narrator's youngest brother
Giovani BATTISTA: Landlord
Hamza HADDAD: Child (Kabar)
Issam KHAN: Richard's friend
Jennifer ROBINS: Event coordinator
Khaled KASSAB: Illegal immigrant
Leo CONTI: Resident (island)
Lia ADAMS: Island investigator
Maria BROWN: Waitress
Muhammad BRAHMANI: Richard's friend
Nader MADANI: Exchange student
Nadia MASRI: Event coordinator
Omran HUSAYN: Immigrant from Feran
Oum Issam: Saghar Psychic
Paul BERNIER: Camilia's French friend
Rahman BOUSTANI: Feran native
Rami FAYAT: Speaker
Rania AHMED: Teacher
Riad RAHAL: Immigrant from Kabar
Richard THOMPSON: Immigrant from Australia
Robert WOLF: Boat captain
Sam GUETTA: Resident of France
Samir TOUMA: Resident of Kabar
Sandra JACKSON: Event coordinator
Wahab HABIB: Saghar immigrant in Italy
William COLINS: Boat crew
Zein MALIK: Richard's friend

## ABOUT THE AUTHOR

Chaker Khazaal is an international spokesperson, human rights advocate, and author. Born in 1987 during the civil war in Lebanon to Palestinian parents, Khazaal grew up in a refugee camp in Beirut. With the highest academic average and strong leadership skills, he was awarded the prestigious Global Leader of Tomorrow Award from York University, Toronto, Canada at the age of seventeen. An accomplished spokesperson on social media, refugee affairs, and global cooperation for developmental projects, he has been invited to venues around the world, such as Google Headquarters and the United Nations. He is regularly featured on-air and in magazines, film, television, and interactive digital media in Canada, the United States of America, the Middle East, and Europe. He has also successfully been published in print media on an international level. After the devastating loss of a friend during the summer of 2012, he began penning his story, which is inspired by the true stories of war children.

Connect with Chaker Khazaal on-line:
    Twitter:    @ChakerKhazaal
    Facebook: fb.com/ChakerKhazaalPage

Made in the USA
Monee, IL
07 December 2019